Dover and the
Claret Tappers

Other Chief Inspector Wilfred Dover Novels
From Foul Play Press

Dover One
Dover Two
Dover Three

Dover and the Claret Tappers

A Detective Chief Inspector
Wilfred Dover Novel

By Joyce Porter

A Foul Play Press Book

The Countryman Press, Inc.
Woodstock, Vermont

X

First U.S. Edition, 1989
Copyright © 1976 by Joyce Porter
First published in Great Britain by Weidenfeld and Nicolson

Library of Congress Cataloging-in-Publication Data

Porter, Joyce.
  Dover and the Claret Tappers : a detective chief inspector Wilfred
Dover novel / by Joyce Porter. — 1st U.S. ed.
      p. cm.
  "A Foul Play Press book."
  "First published in Great Britain by Weidenfeld and Nicolson"-
-T.p. verso.
  ISBN 0-88150-148-4
  I. Title.
PRS066.O72D69 1989   89-15784
823'.914—dc20   CIP

Printed in the United States of America

A Foul Play Press Book
The Countryman Press, Inc.
Woodstock, Vermont
05091

To Bunty Giddens,
With all best wishes and much affection.

One

The news spread through Scotland Yard like wildfire. Ordinary constables had heard the rumours by ten o'clock and by the end of the mid-morning coffee break the sergeants were *au fait* with the situation. From then on the pace accelerated and by lunch-time even the superintendents had caught a whiff of the most amazing development in the fight against crime since they got rid of the Bow Street Runners.

The last person to be told was, of course, the Assistant Commissioner (Crime), the man upon whose desk this particular baby was destined to come home to roost. It was a little after two o'clock when the news was broken to him.

He listened in silence.

'So that's how things stand as of at this particular moment in time, sir,' concluded Commander Brockhurst, head of the Yard's Murder Squad. 'Of course, we're still pursuing our enquiries but I think you'll find that we've got the broad outline more or less accurately drawn.'

The Assistant Commissioner (Crime) peered over the top of his reading glasses at his rock-solid subordinate. 'Now pull the other one, Tom!' he advised jocularly.

'No joke, sir. My lads in the Murder Squad opened a bottle

7

of champagne to celebrate with, and you know they're not the ones to go chucking their money around without good cause.'

The Assistant Commissioner (Crime) was an innate pessimist. 'It's some sort of a hoax, then.'

'That's always a possibility, sir, but I don't think so.' Commander Brockhurst half rose from his chair as he handed a typewritten letter, carefully backed with cardboard and enclosed in a transparent plastic envelope, across the desk. 'In any event, Detective Chief Inspector Dover hasn't been seen since he left the Yard at eight o'clock last night.'

The Assistant Commissioner (Crime) accepted the proffered missive and resumed his nit-picking. 'Well, that sounds as phoney as all hell for a start! What in God's name was Dover supposed to be doing here at eight o'clock at night? And don't tell me he was working!'

Commander Brockhurst allowed himself a grin. 'The popular theory, sir, is that he overslept.'

'What about Mrs Dover?' The Assistant Commissioner (Crime) was running a sceptical eye down the typewritten letter.

'Mrs Dover, sir?'

The Assistant Commissioner (Crime) looked up. 'Well, didn't she notice her beloved Wilf was missing?'

Commander Brockhurst placidly crossed one leg over the other. 'Mrs Dover's not the sort to look a gift horse in the mouth, sir.' he replied a trifle enigmatically. 'She said she just assumed he'd been sent off on a job somewhere when he didn't turn up. He doesn't always bother to phone, I understand.'

'That I can well believe!' sniffed the Assistant Commissioner (Crime). 'Consideration-for-others is *not* Dover's middle name!' He dropped the letter onto his desk. 'It must be a hoax, Tom! I mean, this ransom note or whatever you call it – it's ludicrous. A hundred thousand pounds in used one-pound notes! The release of political prisoners! A manifesto to be read out at peak-viewing hour on the telly! God help us, it reads like something a bunch of school kids would dream up.'

8

'They did send Dover's warrant card with the letter, sir. As proof that they'd actually got him.'

'You didn't tell me that!' The Assistant Commissioner scowled at his subordinate and then prepared to defend his prejudices to the death. 'Well, somebody could have found it somewhere. It wouldn't be the first time Dover's lost his blooming warrant card.'

'Nor the twenty-first.'

'And look at the signature!' The Assistant Commissioner flicked the letter along his desk with a disdainful forefinger. '"The Claret Tappers"! I ask you!'

'I was wondering if that could be a lead,' said Commander Brockhurst thoughtfully.

'A lead?'

'It's an old boxing term, sir. They used to talk about "tapping the claret" when they'd made a man's nose bleed.'

'I am well aware of the sanguinary connotations of the expression "claret tapping", Tom!' snapped the Assistant Commissioner (Crime). 'But, if you think we may be looking for a bunch of anarchistical pugilists, I'm afraid I don't.'

Commander Brockhurst was a great one for taking both life and his superior officers philosophically. 'No, sir,' he said placidly.

The Assistant Commissioner picked up the letter again. 'Well, what do we do now, Tom?'

'I don't think there's much we can do at the moment, sir. From the point of view of further investigations, I mean. In my estimation, we've done about all we can.'

'Oh?'

'We've checked that letter for fingerprints, sir, and there aren't any. Dover's warrant card and the envelope are still down in the lab but I doubt if they'll get anything much off them. The envelope was posted in this part of London between seven-thirty and nine last night and just addressed to "New Scotland Yard". Paper and envelope – cheap, mass-produced stuff you can buy anywhere. Sent first-class post and the stamp moistened with a sponge so we can't even come up with some-body's blood group. These lads aren't making any stupid mistakes, sir.'

'It's all these damned detective stories and cops and robbers on the telly,' grumbled the Assistant Commissioner (Crime). 'The way I see it, you might as well damned well publish a handbook of do's and don'ts for villains.'

Commander Brockhurst knew better than to let his boss climb into the saddle of that particular hobby-horse. 'And I've had a word with Special Branch, sir.'

'Special Branch?' The Assistant Commissioner (Crime) buried his face in his hands. 'Don't tell me you think Dover's been snatched by the agents of some foreign power!'

'I just thought Special Branch might have come across these "Claret Tappers", sir, though I must admit they sound more like one of these pop groups than a subversive political organisation.'

'And had they?'

Commander Brockhurst shook a leonine head. 'Never heard of them, sir. Not that that means anything, apparently. These political groups come and go like mushrooms in a wet field.' Commander Brockhurst's farming antecedents were slightly more remote than he realised. 'The chap in Special Branch was quite intrigued, though. Seems it's the first time anybody's tried to snatch a copper. He reckoned it might start a fashion.' The commander grinned ruefully. 'There's not so much public sympathy for the victim, you see, sir, if they have to bump him off.'

The Assistant Commissioner (Crime) spurned the red her-ring of police/public relations. 'They're sure it's political?'

'What else can it be, sir?' asked Commander Brockhurst, shrugging a pair of very ample shoulders. 'The policeman's a symbol of law and order, a pillar of the Establishment, a willing lackey of the capitalist system. Tailor-made for a job like this, if you ask me.'

The Assistant Commissioner (Crime) was trying to give up

10

smoking. He got his bag of boiled sweets out. 'It could be criminal. D'you want one, Tom? Money the main object, of course, but a touch of revenge mixed in as well.' He selected a pineapple drop and unwrapped it slowly. 'Somebody with a grudge, eh? The underworld' – he perked up visibly as the telling phrase sprang to his lips – 'getting its own back!'

Commander Brockhurst managed to keep his astonishment within bounds. 'On Wilf Dover, sir? To the best of my knowledge, he's been the best friend the underworld's had this century! The man's a crying disgrace to the entire Metropolitan Police Force and the fact that my Murder Squad's had to put up with him all these years is little short of scandalous. I've ...'

'Yes, yes!' The Assistant Commissioner (Crime) had heard all these gripes about Detective Chief Inspector Dover a thousand times before and, if there had been anything to be done about it, he would have done it years ago. The snag was that Dover knew just how far he could go. He was lazy, inefficient, stupid, prone to bullying and probably dishonest, but it is notoriously difficult to get rid of a policeman without some pretty solid proof. It was just this solid proof that Dover, so far, had been canny enough not to provide. In spite of being obscenely overweight, he had elevated the craft of skating on thin ice to a fine art. A thousand times his eager superiors thought they had got him, but a thousand times he emerged, thanks to good luck and low cunning, smelling of roses. The Assistant Commissioner (Crime) sighed. 'You can't tell me anything about Dover that I don't already know. Still, keep your fingers crossed, Tom!' Rather unexpectedly the Assistant Commissioner screwed his face up into a broad wink. 'All may not yet be lost.'

'Sir?'

The Assistant Commissioner suppressed an unworthy thought about none being so blind as those who won't see. 'The mortality rate amongst kidnap victims is extraordinarily high.'

'Ah!' The commander's rubicund face cleared and he

11

returned the Assistant Commissioner's wink. 'All the more reason, if I may say so, sir, for leaving no stone unturned. Just in case our actions are subjected to scrutiny at some later date.'

'Quite.' The Assistant Commissioner frowned and jammed the brakes on his imagination. Alluring as a future without that slob Dover might be, Tom Brockhurst was right – all the motions must be gone through meticulously. 'Now, how do you suggest we handle this reply they want on the telly?'

Commander Brockhurst picked up the typewritten letter again. 'They want a spokesman to appear in the Nine O'Clock News to announce acceptance of their terms for the return of Dover. Hm. That's BBC 1, isn't it? Well, I think we'll have to comply with the demand, sir, if only to give us more time. Er – you'll be the spokesman, will you, sir?'

The Assistant Commissioner (Crime) was very proud of his profile. 'Who else?' He smirked modestly and smoothed his hair down. 'By the way, how's Sergeant MacGregor taking all this?'

'I hear they've had to give him a sedative, sir. He's over the moon. He's had his bellyfull of working with Dover all these years. He puts in an application for transfer at least once a week.'

'Application for transfer to what?' asked the Assistant Commissioner curiously.

'To anything, sir. Last time he wanted to join the Bomb Disposal Squad, if I remember correctly. And before that it was a course for Dog Handlers. You can't really blame him. It can't be any picnic running in double harness with Dover.'

'It's character building!' asserted the Assistant Commissioner who was a hard man. 'The sooner these kids learn that life isn't a bowl of cherries, the better. Now, anything else?'

'No, I don't think so, sir.' Commander Brockhurst collected the plastic-covered letter from the desk where he'd returned it.

'You'll be able to identify the typewriter at any rate.'

'Oh, we've done that already, sir. It's a Parnassus TR 8 and it's taken a fair old battering in its time. We'll know it all right –

12

when we find it.'

'What about the typist?'

'A two-finger job, sir. Fairly nippy but not trained.'

One of the six telephones on the Assistant Commissioner (Crime)'s desk rang imperiously. The Assistant Commissioner lunged for the receiver, motioning Commander Brockhurst to stay where he was. 'The Big White Chief!' he hissed.

The telephone conversation which ensued was lengthy but one-sided. The Assistant Commissioner's part – and it was definitely not type-casting – was restricted to a string of obsequious 'yes-sirs' and 'no-sirs'. Commander Brockhurst passed the time trying to guess what was being said at the other end of the crackling wire.

There was a final 'yes-sir-very-good-sir-at-once-sir' and a ragged Assistant Commissioner dropped the receiver back in its cradle. 'Bloody hell!' he gasped.

'Trouble, sir?'

'With a capital T, Tom. Somebody's tipped the bloody press off. The Commissioner's up there, blowing his top off. Besieged in his office – or so he says – by a horde of hungry newspaper men.'

Commander Brockhurst rose to his feet again. 'It was only a matter of time, sir. The whole world's going to know what's happened when you make your broadcast this evening. Besides, the publicity may help us. After all, somebody may have seen something.'

The Assistant Commissioner (Crime) stood up, too, and retrieved his boiled sweetie from the ashtray. 'It's not really the fact that somebody's let the cat out of the bag that's got him wetting his pants. The Home Secretary's been on the blower. He wants us both round to the Home Office for a conference. It seems that Dover's kidnapping has become a political issue.'

'In that case,' said Commander Brockhurst with a grimace, 'Mrs Dover might as well start ordering her widow's weeds now. Old Wilf's chances of coming out of this with a whole skin were pretty dim right from the beginning, but if the bloody politicians are going to start meddling he hasn't got a snowball's.'

The Assistant Commissioner (Crime) crunched his boiled sweet. 'It's an ill wind,' he remarked as he went to get his overcoat off the stand. 'You'd better stand by at eight o'clock tonight, Tom, to give me a briefing before I go on the air. There may be some last-minute development I should know about.'

'Right you are, sir!' Commander Brockhurst opened the door and the Assistant Commissioner (Crime) swept through it with all the panache of a man on his way to higher things.

At exactly nine o'clock the merry jingle which heralds the news on BBC television rang out in countless sitting-rooms. The countless viewers reacted to the arrival of their daily dose of gloom and misery in several ways. Some leapt as though shot from their fireside chairs and rushed off to make a cup of tea or pay a visit to the toilet. Others bestirred themselves only to the extent of stretching out an arm and switching smartly to the other channel. The rest – the optimists, the masochists and the fast asleep – sat it out and so had the thrill of hearing that some as yet unidentified terrorist group had kidnapped a detective chief inspector from New Scotland Yard. A photograph of Dover that was well-nigh actionable flashed up on the screen and a middle-aged housewife in South Shields summed up the majority verdict: 'Cripes, if he looks like that, they're welcome to him!'

The newscaster chattered on. He was looking quite excited as he prepared to play his small part in a piece of television history.

'In a letter setting out their demands,' he said, 'the kidnappers gave instructions on the method to be used for getting in touch with them. A senior police officer was to appear on the Nine O'Clock News and publicly accept their terms. The BBC is pleased to offer the hospitality of its studios to the Assistant Commissioner for Crime at New Scotland Yard!'

The scene changed and the watching world was treated to

14

the spectacle of a very spruced up Assistant Commissioner leering happily down the cleavage of the young lady who had been specially selected to interview him. The young lady picked up her cue and turned smoothly to smile at the camera.

'Assistant Commissioner, you and your colleagues at New Scotland Yard must have been very shocked and distressed when you realised that Detective Chief Inspector Dover had been kidnapped by a gang of urban guerillas?'

The Assistant Commissioner tore his eyes away and, in something of a panic, tried to remember his lines. Damn and blast the little harpy, why couldn't she have warned him they were going on the air! 'Er – yes,' he spluttered. 'Quite.'

'As a member of Scotland Yard's famous Murder Squad, Chief Inspector Dover must have made many enemies amongst the criminal classes. Do you think that this could be an attempt to pay off an old score?'

'Er – no,' said the Assistant Commissioner, adding quickly while he'd the chance to get a word in, 'though we are naturally leaving no avenue unexplored and no – er – theory uninvestigated.'

The young lady interviewer nodded her head mechanically. She was there to ask questions, not listen to a bunch of boring old answers. 'So, in spite of the fact that the kidnappers are demanding a ransom of one hundred thousand pounds for the safe return of Chief Inspector Dover, the authorities are working on the assumption that there is a political motive behind the crime?'

'Er – yes.' The Assistant Commissioner (Crime) was not best pleased at having a nubile, teenage moppet up-stage him. 'There were, of course, other demands besides the – er – money.'

The young lady interviewer, greatly daring, ventured a spontaneous query. 'What other demands?'

The Assistant Commissioner smiled a superior little smile. 'I'm afraid I'm not at liberty to reveal that at this stage in the proceedings.' Having been able to spurn a perfectly reason-

15

able request for information he began to feel much better.

'Is Chief Inspector Dover or his family in a position to pay a ransom of one hundred thousand pounds for his safe return?'

'Certainly not!'

'Could police funds of any kind be made available?'

The Assistant Commissioner's eyes all but popped out of his head. 'What police funds?'

'I don't know,' said the young lady interviewer rather crossly. 'I'm asking you. I mean, where do the kidnappers think the money's coming from?'

'You'd better ask them!' came the tart, if inevitable, answer.

The young lady interviewer's brow lowered and she was just about to give back as good as she was getting when she caught the producer's frantic winding-up signals. God knows, there was more to life than missing policemen and there was that strike of dental surgeons in Gwent to fit in, to say nothing of the usual economic stuff and Bobby Buxton's world shattering transfer from Liverpool to Everton for a reputed fee of two million...

'I believe you have an announcement that you wish to make to the kidnappers of Detective Chief Inspector Dover,' snapped the young lady interviewer, her bosom (to which she owed so much of her success on the box) heaving sulkily as she scowled at the Assistant Commissioner. Dirty old lecher!

'I have, indeed!' The Assistant Commissioner, not realising that he was *hors de combat* in that particular sex war, straightened up as the cameras zoomed in on him. The watching audience got him full faced and naturally assumed that the faint smile playing round his lips was an indication of kindly benevolence. In a way, of course, it was: the Assistant Commissioner reckoned that what he was about to do was the best thing that had happened to the Metropolitan Police since the introduction of the whistle in 1884. Raising his chin, he let Number One camera have it straight in the lens.

'I am speaking now,' he began, 'to those criminals who have been so foolish and misguided as to kidnap Detective Chief

Inspector Dover, a valued colleague of mine ... and a friend.'
The Assistant Commissioner gagged a bit over this but he got it
out. 'I call upon them to release Wilfred Dover, their innocent
victim, and return him unharmed and without delay to the
bosom of his distressed family. Because, whatever you in your
greed may think, crime does not pay – and this particular crime
will certainly not pay. The combined might of every police
force in this country will see to that and, sooner or later, you
will be relentlessly hounded down and brought before the bar
of British Justice!' The Assistant Commissioner had learnt this
stirring speech off by heart and didn't need more than the odd
glance at the teleprompter to refresh his memory. 'Your
punishment will be heavy. Don't make it even more severe by
daring to harm one hair of Wilf Dover's head! For I have to tell
you that neither Her Majesty's government nor the Metropolitan Police is prepared to make any compromise in this matter.
The conclusion has been reached, after much anguished heart
searching, that to submit to threats of this nature is merely to
invite further incidents of moral blackmail. Let me make the
position crystal clear and tell you that our decision is final and
irrevocable. None of your conditions for the safe release of
Chief Inspector Dover from his durance vile will be met. Not
one! We will not allow you to broadcast your so-called political
manifesto. We will not release any so-called political prisoners
from the jails where they are so justly serving heavy prison
sentences for their crimes. And, lastly but by no means leastly,
we will not pay a ransom of one hundred thousand pounds or
any other sum of money, however trivial.'

The Assistant Commissioner, who was beginning to sweat a
little under the lights, paused dramatically to let his words sink
in. Out of sight of the cameras pandemonium was breaking out.
Everybody had been so sure, for some reason, that the Assistant Commissioner had come to capitulate to the demands of
the kidnappers that nobody had actually bothered to ask him
what he was going to say. The producer had merely implored
him, as he implored every spokesman, to 'try and keep it nice

17

and short, lovie!' The mimed panic soon resolved itself into a battle of wills between the distraught producer and the nubile young lady interviewer. He wanted her to resume her interrogation of the Assistant Commissioner in the face of this startling new development but she was determined not to appear before the cameras without a list of carefully prepared questions securely affixed to her clip-board. She was a conceited girl but, where her intellectual abilities were concerned, she recognised her limitations. The producer, although he was by no means the sort of man to lay hands lightly on a woman, was preparing to resort to physical coercion when the Assistant Commissioner continued with his oration.

'So, in conclusion, let me appeal to you most sincerely to abandon this terrible plan. Release Chief Inspector Dover! You will gain nothing, either now or in the future, by continuing to detain him. Forget your brutal threats! Don't get yourselves into any more trouble than you are in already. Believe me, if you so much as lay a finger on Wilf Dover, you will receive no mercy when we catch up with you – as catch up with you we most surely will. Thank you – and goodnight!'

There was an awkward pause and then the producer, gratefully releasing his hold on the young lady interviewer and biting back his tears, flapped a limp hand at the news reader.

Number Two camera came up and life went on. 'The strike of dental surgeons in Gwent has, according to a statement issued by their association, already begun to bite . . .'

Up in South Shields the middle-aged housewife spoke for us all. 'Well,' she chuckled as she nudged her husband into semi-wakefulness, 'fancy that!'

Two

The three Claret Tappers sat staring at the talking heads, too stunned to move.

At last the first kidnapper bestirred himself. 'Switch that bloody thing off!'

The third kidnapper, the one at the bottom of the pecking order, hurried to obey. The screen went dead.

The second kidnapper was chicken. 'They're having us on, aren't they?'

'Bloody hell!' The first kidnapper's mind was roaring away like a Formula One car. If he didn't watch it, he'd have the whole bloody business coming apart in his hands.

The second kidnapper was desperate for reassurance. 'It's a bluff, isn't it? They're trying to con us.'

'Oh, belt up, for Christ's sake! I'm trying to bloody think.'

The third kidnapper was as white as a sheet. 'How are we going to do it? I mean, he's a big man. He isn't just going to sit there and ...'

'Shut up, the bloody pair of you!' The first kidnapper sucked in a great mouthful of air and tried to calm down. 'Look,' he said, speaking more quietly, 'we've got to check this.'

'Check?'

'That' – the first kidnapper jerked a would-be contemptuous thumb at the television set – 'could be for the birds. Keeping up the public's morale or something. The pigs just don't want to lose face, that's all. Don't you sweat – they'll negotiate behind the scenes.'

His companions continued to look like a pair of cream-faced loons.

'You never said what we was to do if they didn't cough the cash up,' Number Three accused his leader miserably. 'You said they'd pay for sure. Oh, God, I don't think I can kill anybody!'

'You won't have to!' The chief Claret Tapper swung round angrily on his second-in-command, a broken reed if ever there was one but all he'd got. He pulled a handful of small change out of his pocket. 'Here, go and phone your sister!'

'Eh?' The second kidnapper backed away from the proffered money as though it carried the plague. 'Ring Jean? What for?'

'To find out what's going on, of course. She'll know if the pigs are trying to pull a fast one, won't she? Oh, go on! Get moving!'

The second kidnapper fought a craven rear-guard action. 'I don't fancy ringing the Yard right now,' he whined. 'Suppose they get suspicious?'

'Why the bloody hell should they? They'll have enough to worry about without getting their knickers in a twist over some bloody girl getting a private telephone call when she's on duty. If anybody asks you – which they bloody won't – tell 'em your old grannie's just up and kicked it.'

The second kidnapper was still hovering by the door. 'What are you going to do?'

The first kidnapper scowled. Sometimes he couldn't help longing for a bit of this blind, unthinking obedience you were always reading about. 'I'm going to sit here, mate,' he said grimly, 'and think until the bloody ten o'clock news comes on the telly.'

20

The second kidnapper came back into the centre of the room. 'You think they'll change their minds?' he asked eagerly. 'You think there'll be another announcement and ...'

'For Christ's sake,' screamed the first kidnapper who merely hid his worries better than his companions, 'sod off!'

The producer of commercial television's ten o'clock news programme had worked himself up into a fair old paddy. He had, as a matter of routine, watched the rival newscast on the BBC at nine o'clock and the sheer, lousy unfairness of it all had got him down and chewing the carpet. Why had old Auntie BBC been handed this wonderful kidnapped copper story on an effing plate while the poor bleeding Independents were expected to scratch around on their own and make do with the left-overs.

'O.K.,' he bellowed eventually at the crowd of technicians, news-readers, secretaries and sycophants who had gathered round him in an orgy of commiseration, 'if that's the way they want to play it, we'll show 'em!' He reached for his telephone before pausing to toss a sop to his megalomania. 'I'll show 'em!'

And, to his credit, he did.

There was a bigger than usual audience for commercial television that evening owing to the fact that the alternative viewing was something less than compulsive. BBC 1 had a forty-five minute profile of one of the more boring and most dogmatic of trade union leaders while BBC 2 was showing its award winning film, *A Day in the Life of the Narrow-Bordered Bee Hawk Moth,* for the third time – and almost anything was better than that.

The producer of News at Ten hadn't been able to achieve the completely impossible, of course. Both the Prime Minister and the Home Secretary had declined invitations to appear at thirty minutes' notice to explain their policy in respect of the outrageous kidnapping of a valued public servant, but Commander Brockhurst, head of the Murder Squad and Dover's immediate

21

superior, was only too happy to oblige. As he told his wife later, for that sort of money he would have appeared in *A Day in the Life of the Narrow-Bordered Bee Hawk Moth*.

After a short résumé of the story so far, Commander Brockhurst came up on the screen, looking the very epitome of your pink and cuddly neighbourhood policeman. The interviewer had been instructed to go hard for the human angle.

'How, Commander Brockhurst, do you think Chief Inspector Dover is feeling at this moment?'

The commander squirmed uneasily. 'Well, I don't suppose he's feeling too chirpy,' he admitted with evident reluctance, 'but...'

'Chief Inspector Dover has been snatched from the very heart of London by a gang of ruthless terrorists and held to ransom. Even where there is a readiness to pay the ransom, the victim of a kidnapping is all too frequently killed. What do you imagine Chief Inspector Dover's thoughts are tonight, when he knows that there has been a blank refusal to bargain in any way with his captors?'

Commander Brockhurst had had time to collect his thoughts. 'Well, I dare say old Wilf Dover will be feeling a bit on the anxious side but he'll be sustained by the knowledge that all his colleagues and chums in the Met will be working twenty-four hours a day to secure his safe release.' Commander Brockhurst risked a surreptitious glance up at the studio ceiling. So far it seemed to be holding firm.

'Won't Chief Inspector Dover consider, though, that the community has betrayed him?' pressed the interviewer. 'That same community, moreover, that he has devoted his life to protecting.'

Commander Brockhurst's mind boggled slightly at the idea of Dover devoting his life to anything other than his own comfort, but he picked up the thread of his platitudes smoothly enough. 'Old Wilf is a professional policeman,' he assured the watching millions heartily, 'and, like the rest of us, he's used to taking the rough with the smooth. He'll appreciate – as every

22

thinking person in the country must – that a line has got to be drawn somewhere. The police have been advocating a tougher policy for years. The only way to get rid of these mindless thugs is to stamp on them – and stamp on them hard. Nobody is more sorry than I am that Wilf Dover is destined to be the guinea pig in this experiment but I know the man and there'll be no whining or complaining from him.'

Out of camera range the producer, getting bored with Commander Brockhurst's stout determination to be brave at some other poor bugger's expense, began to make his wind-it-up signs.

Commander Brockhurst got in one last gesture from the Boy's Own Paper code. Raising his thumb to the camera he grinned cheerfully. 'Chins up, Dover!' he counselled, and his use of the plural was a perfectly understandable Freudian slip.

The newscaster was flashing his teeth again. 'We're going to take a short break now,' he announced as though it was some kind of special treat, 'but after the break we shall be bringing you an interview with Chief Inspector Dover's wife, as well as the latest news on the dentists' strike in Wales and Bobby Buxton on what it feels like to be worth two million pounds.' The eyes crinkled appealingly. 'Join us then!'

For connoisseurs of the human condition, Mrs Dover was a treat worth waiting for. She had been filmed earlier on in the evening in her own kitchen and she appeared on the screen looking astonishingly bright and cheerful. By a fortunate coincidence she had paid her monthly visit to the hairdresser's that very morning and now faced the world from under a passing fair imitation of a corrugated iron roof. There had been some vague idea at first that she should be filmed performing some trivial domestic chore – like ironing her husband's pyjamas. That, of course, had been before the television people had actually seen Dover's pyjamas. When they had, they decided not to bother.

Mrs Dover was experiencing some difficulty in stopping talking. It only needed one word from her interlocutor and she

23

was off, nineteen to the dozen. Yes, shocked simply wasn't the word for what she'd felt when they'd told her that Wilfred had been kidnapped. She'd gone weak at the knees, really. And everything had started to go quite black and ... No, of course she'd never imagined her husband would ever be so silly as to go and get himself kidnapped! Why on earth should she? The idea had never even crossed her mind. Things like that just simply didn't happen to people like them and ... Well, yes, naturally she was worried about him because, quite apart from anything else, his health wasn't all that good and he was terribly prone to chills on the stomach and ... Eh? Oh, yes, she did appeal to the kidnappers, wherever and whoever they might be, to let her husband go.

It was at this point that careful watchers might have detected a slight diminution in Mrs Dover's sparkling good humour. The prospect of her husband's safe return made her look fractionally less like a football pools winner than heretofore.

The interviewer carried on. 'What do you think, Mrs Dover, about the decision of the authorities to refuse absolutely and entirely to compromise with the chief inspector's abductors? Don't you feel it grossly unfair that your husband's life should be put at risk in this way?'

'Well ...' Mrs Dover vacillated and pleated her best frock with nervous fingers. 'Well ...' She took a deep breath and started again. 'They did explain it to me and I can quite see their point of view, you know. I mean, you can't let this sort of thing go on for ever, can you? You've got to take a stand somewhere, don't you? It's just Wilfred's hard luck that ...' Mrs Dover's voice trailed off.

'Quite!' The interviewer was shown nodding sympathetically in a shot that had been filmed half an hour after the interview had ended.

Mrs Dover smiled shyly. 'A hundred thousand pounds is quite a lot of money,' she pointed out.

'Indeed! Yes, I think we would all agree with that. And now, Mrs Dover, what are your plans for the immediate future?'

'Oh, well, now I've been thinking about that. I shall pack in this place, of course, and move in with my younger sister. She's got ever such a nice little house down in Essex and she's a widow, too, so there'll be plenty of room for me and my bits and pieces there.'

The interviewer was a little confused. 'Temporarily, you mean? Just while you're waiting for news about your husband's fate?' he asked.

Mrs Dover smiled forgivingly at the silly boy. 'Oh, no,' she said, her earlier cheerfulness breaking through again, 'I mean permanently. For good. I wouldn't dream, of course,' she added virtuously, 'of leaving this house until after the funeral, though. Well, it wouldn't be right, would it?'

It was three o'clock in the morning and the Claret Tappers were still sitting round a television set that had been cold and dead for hours. The air was thick with smoke and they were down to the last two cans of brown ale.

The first kidnapper's voice was quite hoarse. 'Look, we've got to make our minds up quick. Every minute we keep him here is another minute of bloody danger for us. Either way, we've got to bloody well get rid of him.'

The brown ale had given the second kidnapper a modicum of dutch courage. 'So we croak him,' he said. 'That's the safest.' He giggled. 'Dead men tell no tales!'

The first kidnapper regarded his confederate wearily. 'Why don't you try using your loaf for a change?' he asked. 'Suppose we do kill him – what do we do with the bloody body? There's over seventeen stone of him, you know. That'll take some shifting.'

'So we leave him here.'

'But this place could lead them to us, couldn't it, you nit? We're bound to leave some clues behind us, no matter how careful we are – especially with silly buggers like you messing about. Well, it's a risk I'm not going to bloody take. We'll dump Dover somewhere. That way they'll never find this place and we may even be able to use it again next time.'

The third kidnapper looked up, arms clasped round his knees in an effort to keep the night's chill out. 'Is there going to be a next time?'

'Too right there is! The reasons we had for going into this in the first place haven't changed, have they?' The first kidnapper's anger showed in his heightened colour and sparkling eyes. 'Just because this one's blown up in our bloody faces, it doesn't mean we're going to chuck our hand in once and for all.'

'No,' murmured the third kidnapper. 'Course not.'

The second kidnapper was less submissive. 'And who's going to cough up a hundred thousand nicker next time?' he jeered. 'They'll bust a gut laughing at us. I'm telling you, mate – if we let this Dover slob go, nobody'll ever take us seriously again.'

This aspect of their predicament had not escaped the first kidnapper and he had, indeed, been sweating over it for hours. In the end he'd succeeded in producing a rationalisation which satisfied him and all he had to do now was sell it to his downcast and disappointed companions. He had to convince them that, in spite of some evidence to the contrary, everything was for the best in the best of all possible worlds and that his hand was still steady on the tiller. 'Trust you to go and get the wrong end of the bloody stick!' he sneered. 'You're so thick you can't see beyond the end of your bloody snout.'

'I can see that we're going to look a right bunch of charlies!' retorted Number Two. 'What's the good of making threats if you don't carry 'em out?'

The first kidnapper leaned forward in his chair and adopted a more conciliatory tone. 'Listen, what's your main stumbling block when it comes to getting your hands on the ransom money, eh?' He saw the second kidnapper's mouth begin to open and rushed hurriedly on. 'I'll tell you, mate! It's convincing the victim's family and friends that you're on the level. Right? It's making 'em believe the chap you've snatched will

26

be returned safe and sound if only they'll cooperate and do what they're told.'

'Blimey, I should have thought that was the least of your worries,' grumbled the second kidnapper, lighting yet another cigarette.

'Well, it isn't! That's just the time the pigs get their foot in the door, isn't it? They tell the family that it's odds on their nearest and dearest has already been croaked and so they might as well play ball with the cops and help catch the naughty kidnappers.'

'What the hell are you supposed to be getting at?'

Mercifully the first kidnapper cut the cackle. 'Simply this – because we've shown ourselves reasonable and humane this time, the next time the victim's family will catch on that there's a good chance of getting their loved one back in one piece, see? Well, that could be bloody important for us. With that sort of hope there will be less temptation to go running to the cops.'

The second kidnapper was still sceptical. 'So this Dover cock-up is really a blessing in disguise?'

'It could be.'

'Jesus.'

'You'll see!'

The second kidnapper blew out a lungful of smoke. 'I dunno why you ever picked this Dover pig in the first place,' he complained. 'He's an effing dead loss, if ever there was one. You might have guessed nobody'd shell out tuppence to get him back. I know I wouldn't. Jean said he was a right old layabout and they've been trying to get shot of him for years. And he's only supernumerary on the Murder Squad, you know. They got lumbered with him back in the year dot and then found they couldn't get rid of him. Nobody else'll have him.'

The third kidnapper risked a sour comment. 'Now he tells us!'

The second kidnapper stamped heavily on this flicker of insubordination. 'My sister told us all this right at the bloody beginning. More or less, anyhow.'

'Precisely!' The first kidnapper gathered up the reins again. 'And that's why we picked him, isn't it? Exactly because he is a great fat, greasy, overweight slob who's not got enough bloody gumption to take shelter when it rains. I don't remember you lot being exactly keen on snatching one of these six-foot-four, keep-fit fanatics with muscles like bloody whipcord.'

The third kidnapper yawned and went off at a tangent. 'Me, I'll be glad to see the back of him. Moan, moan, moan - ever since he got here. He'd have you waiting on him hand and foot if you gave him half a chance. Always trying to cadge cigarettes - and eat? I'm telling you, I've had it up to here cooking food for that pig and doing all the washing up after him, too.'

The yawn was catching. The second kidnapper all but dislocated his jaw. 'My heart bleeds for you, kiddo!' he grunted. 'Still, we've got more important things on our plate than your effing life and hard times. What I say is - if we're going to dump Dover, let's dump him quick!'

'Haven't I been telling you that for bloody hours?' The first kidnapper picked up one of the beer cans and shook it hopefully. It was empty. 'The thing is - how?'

'What about the scheme we was saving for when the ransom had been paid?'

The first kidnapper stared thoughtfully at the third. 'I suppose so. Anybody got a better idea?'

Nobody had.

The first kidnapper sighed and stretched himself. He stood up. 'Come on, then! Let's do it now and get it over with. Then we can go to bed. I'm bloody shagged.'

Number Two pulled himself to his feet. He dragged his pullover up and extracted a gun from the waist-belt of his jeans. 'And I'll tell you something else,' he said as he followed the others from the room. 'Next time I'm going to get myself a *real* shooter! I feel a right twit, toting a bleeding kid's toy around.'

It was eight-thirty on Thursday morning. Victoria Street was crowded but Detective Sergeant MacGregor picked his way through the hurrying office workers and shop assistants with a light heart and a nimble foot. My, my – but life was *good*! For the first time for many a long and dreary year Sergeant MacGregor was actually looking forward to the day's work, though he was finding it hard to visualise what things would be like without Dover's peevish, obtuse and sullen personality dominating the scene.

Oh, well, who cared about the details? It would be simply marvellous, that was for sure. MacGregor swung his black leather gents' handbag happily from his wrist. It was the first day he'd ever dared bring it to the Yard but he felt the occasion of Dover's thrice-blessed dissolution merited something more than that by way of celebration. MacGregor mulled the problem over as he floated on Cloud Nine down Broadway and up the steps of New Scotland Yard. It was only when he was in the lift that the ideal solution struck him. He'd buy himself a new hat! A hand-made, custom-built, curly-brimmed bowler to wear at Dover's funeral!

MacGregor was still sniggering happily over the felicity of his plan when he reported half an hour later to Commander Brockhurst's office.

'You wanted to see me, sir?'

Commander Brockhurst glanced at MacGregor's happy, smiling face and sighed. 'You'd better sit down, sergeant.'

'Thank you, sir!' It was going to take a sledge-hammer to wipe the grin off MacGregor's face.

Regretfully, the commander wielded it. 'They've found Chief Inspector Dover,' he said. 'Done up in a plastic sack and dumped round the back of the Old Bailey with the rest of the rubbish. It was the dustbin men who found him.'

MacGregor was surprised. 'Gosh, sir,' he said, 'these Claret Tappers don't hang about, do they? It's less than twelve hours since the Assistant Commissioner made his announcement on the television and here they've gone and killed poor old ...'

'Sergeant,' interrupted Commander Brockhurst, firmly but

29

compassionately, 'Chief Inspector Dover isn't dead.'

There was an anguished pause.

'Isn't dead, sir?' queried MacGregor from a throat that had suddenly gone dry.

'Far from it,' said the commander who had already received a formal complaint from the dustbin men's trade union representative about some of Dover's remarks to his rescuers. 'There doesn't appear to be a scratch on him.'

MacGregor made the supreme effort. 'Good,' he murmured.

'We've sent him to hospital for observation, though, just in case. They'll probably keep him in till tomorrow.'

'Till tomorrow,' repeated MacGregor, trying to extract what comfort he could from that.

Commander Brockhurst, feeling that the worst was now over, shuffled some papers briskly on his desk. 'Still, you'd better get over and see him right away. I want these kidnappers caught, sergeant, and no messing about. It's bad for our image, having senior detectives snatched off the streets of London. I'm putting Chief Inspector Dover, himself, in charge of the investigation, of course.' For a brief second Commander Brockhurst let his official manner slip. His eyes twinkled. 'At least the old devil won't suffer from lack of motivation *this* time!'

Three

The frosty glare that MacGregor got from the girl on the reception desk told him that Dover had already left his mark (and it was probably an indelible one) on St Basil's Hospital. Feeling pretty depressed, the sergeant made his way as slowly as he dared along the echoing corridors and up the chilly, uncarpeted stairs. All too soon he reached his objective and pushed open the door of the private room in which, not surprisingly, Dover had been put. Even in the Health Service, some consideration is shown for the welfare and comfort of the sick.

''Strewth,' growled Dover in lieu of greeting, 'you've taken your blooming time, haven't you?'

'They wouldn't let me in before, sir,' explained MacGregor. 'They said you hadn't got to be disturbed.' It was a black lie of course but those who associate with Dover soon get used to bartering their immortal souls for a quiet life. MacGregor pulled up a chair to the bedside. 'You're looking frightfully fit, sir!' This was true. Arrayed in a clean pair of hospital pyjamas and having been forcibly bathed by a nursing sister who campaigned for compulsory vasectomies for all males over the age of sixteen, Dover did indeed look strikingly more delectable than usual. Medical science hadn't had time to do anything for

such fundamentals as pernicious dandruff, chronic embon-
point and acute dyspepsia but the general impression was still
extremely creditable.

The last thing that Scotland Yard's most accomplished lead
swinger and scrimshanker wanted to hear was that he was
looking fit for duty. Dover twitched his little black moustache
and tried a touch of pathos. 'Haven't you brought me any
bloody grapes or anything?'

MacGregor hadn't.

Dover brushed aside the lame excuses. 'Oh, give us a fag,
then!'

MacGregor hadn't been fool enough to bring his little
handbag to the hospital so he produced his cigarettes from his
pocket in the normal way and soon had Dover puffing smoke all
round the room and covering the top sheet with ash. Dover's
hand closed like a vice round the cigarette packet.

'I'll hang onto this,' he said.

MacGregor sighed. 'Don't they come round with one of
those trollies where you can buy things, sir?' he asked without
much hope.

'Got no money,' explained Dover, slipping the cigarettes
under his pillow. 'Those thugs robbed me, you know. Nicked
every penny I had on me – apart from the pound note I keep in
my sock for emergencies. I reckon somebody ought to reim-
burse me.'

Very slowly, so as not to frighten his lord and master,
MacGregor was pulling his notebook out. 'You might try
claiming it on your swindle sheet, sir,' he suggested helpfully.
'How much was it?'

'Sixty-four pence!' said Dover promptly. Too promptly!
With a bit more pause for thought, he admonished himself
crossly, he could have upped that to thousands of pounds.

MacGregor cautiously extracted a pencil. 'What exactly
happened, sir?'

Dover looked blank.

'When you were kidnapped, sir. Commander Brockhurst

was rather keen that we should get cracking on the investigation without delay.'

It would be an exaggeration to say that these unkind and thoughtless remarks brought the tears to Dover's eyes, but they certainly brought a howl of protest to his lips. 'Is there no bloody consideration?' he yelled. 'Damn it all, I'm supposed to be ill! By rights I ought to be lying down under sedation in a darkened room, not sitting here being third-degreed by some young whelp of a jack who isn't dry yet behind the bloody ears!'

There was a great deal more in the same vein but eventually Dover succumbed to the temptation to star in his own drama. He wasn't indifferent, either, to the sweetness of revenge on the cheeky bastards who'd abducted him. 'Tuesday night, it was,' he began, leaning back amongst his pillows and closing his eyes. 'I'd been working late at the Yard, clearing up the paperwork and things.' His eyes snapped open and he glared accusingly at MacGregor. 'Doing your blooming work, as it happens, laddie!' He stabbed out a grubby-nailed forefinger. 'Do you realise that, if you hadn't gone skiving off on one of these stupid courses of yours, none of this might ever have happened?'

MacGregor refused to feel guilty. 'You left the Yard about eight o'clock, didn't you sir? What happened then?'

'I was just walking to the station to catch a train home when, after I'd gone a hundred yards or so, this taxi pulls up at the kerb just ahead of me. The door opens and a chap sort of half leans out and shouts, "Can I give you a lift, Dover?" Well, naturally, I shouted "Yes!" back and put on a bit of a spurt so's not to keep the chap waiting.'

MacGregor was amazed at such consideration for the convenience of others but he made, of course, no comment.

Dover sank back and closed his eyes again. 'So, I start to get into the taxi - see? - and that's when it struck me that there was something fishy going on.'

'Oh?'

Dover yawned. 'Hm.'

'What?'

'Eh?'

MacGregor counted up to ten and thus managed to keep his hands to himself. 'What made you think something was wrong, sir?'

Dover opened his eyes and regarded MacGregor resentfully. 'I ought to be in bed, you know,' he grizzled.

'You *are* in bed, sir!'

Dover scowled.

'What was the "something fishy", sir?' MacGregor displayed bulldog tenacity but he was no match for Dover.

'Can't remember!' said Dover with an evil grin. Pretty boy would have to get up a hell of a lot earlier in the morning to catch *him* napping! 'Now, where was I?'

MacGregor hoisted the white flag. 'You were just getting into the taxicab, sir.'

'That's right! Well, it was dark, you know, and I was sort of trying to see who this chap sitting there was. Then, suddenly, I felt something poke me in the back. Another fellow had come creeping up behind me! He gave me another poke and told me to get right into the taxi or he'd blow my bloody brains out.'

MacGregor looked up. 'Can you recall his exact words, sir?'

'You've a hope! You try going around with a gun stuck in your back and see how much you remember.'

'How about the gun, sir? Did you happen to notice what make it was?'

Dover shook his head. 'Soon as I got in the taxi, they jumped me, didn't they? I fought 'em off, of course, but they overpowered me in the end and I was bound hand and foot and dumped on the floor. Then the lousy yobboes shoved some sticking plaster over my mouth and dragged a mucky old sack over my head and that was that. I dare say,' added Dover with a heavy sneer, 'that a clever young devil like you would have burst free and escaped in a couple of bloody shakes, but I couldn't quite manage it.'

34

MacGregor very sensibly ignored the jibe and concentrated on extracting as much information as he could from Dover's rather hazy reminiscences. 'So there were three men involved at this stage, sir?'

'Two!' Dover corrected him nastily. 'Why don't you wash your lugholes out? One on the back seat and one with the gun.'

'There was another man driving the taxi, though, wasn't there, sir?'

Dover was frankly disgusted at such finickiness. 'Oh, well, if you're going to count him ...'

MacGregor stared rigidly at his notebook. One day, he promised himself, one day he was going to grab that fat, ill-natured slob by the throat and choke the living daylights out of him. *Slowly!*

Dover, unprompted for once, resumed his story. 'Then we drove off. From start to finish I don't reckon the whole business of snatching me took more than a minute at the outside. Oh, I'm telling you – those boys were professionals, all right! As slick and ruthless as they come. I didn't stand a chance. Well, eventually we arrived at our destination and it's no bloody good you asking me where it was because I don't know. I told you, I was gagged and blindfolded. Well, I was forced out of the taxi – at gun point, mind you – and hurried into a building of some sort and taken upstairs. Then they made me lie face down on the floor.' Dover's bottom lip protruded disconsolately as he recalled the indignities to which he had been subjected. 'They untied my hands and the next thing I heard was a door being slammed and locked. I waited till everything had gone quiet and then I pulled the bag off my head and removed that damned sticking-plaster.' Dover felt tenderly at his little black moustache. 'And then I had a rest. The room I was in was dark so, when I'd got my circulation going again, I started groping about until I found an electric light switch. I switched it on and discovered that I'd been incarcerated in a small room with no windows.'

MacGregor's pencil paused in its mad rush over the paper.

'A cupboard, sir?'

'No, not a cupboard!' said Dover tartly. 'A small room. And now,' – he folded his arms resolutely – 'you'd better nip outside and organise some coffee because you're not going to get another cheep out of me till I've wet my whistle. It's blooming dry work, all this talking.'

It took MacGregor longer than he would have believed to bribe and cajole a pot of coffee and a few biscuits out of a most uncooperative hospital staff. In the end, more by good luck than judgement, he chanced upon a blackleg who was prepared to sacrifice her most deeply held principles for hard cash. 'And you want to think yourself lucky,' she informed MacGregor as she shoved a tray swimming with spilt coffee into his hands, 'that it isn't laced with arsenic!'

MacGregor managed to direct the stream of coffee away from his trousers. 'Oh, come now,' he chided his benefactress, 'things can't be as bad as all that, surely? He's only been here a few hours.'

'And, if he's here for many more, sonnie,' – the tea-lady's curlers wobbled menacingly under her headscarf – 'there'll be ructions that'll leave your head ringing!'

MacGregor woke Dover up again, plumped his pillows for him, poured out his coffee and sugared it, and finally lit another cigarette for him. In return Dover grudgingly consented to answer a few questions.

'These kidnappers, sir,' began MacGregor, consulting his notes without much hope. 'Can you tell me a bit more about them? What age were they, for example?'

Dover thought about it. 'Mid-twenties, p'raps. Like I told you, I barely clapped eyes on 'em.'

'Tall? Short? Fat? Thin?'

'Medium,' said Dover firmly.

'All of them, sir?'

Dover nodded his head and gave most of his attention to spooning some soggy biscuit out of the depths of his coffee cup.

MacGregor was past sighing. 'What about their voices, sir?'

'Nobody said more than half a dozen words to me the whole time.'

'But the man who invited you into the taxi, sir? Had he got an accent of any sort? Was it a cultured voice or ...?'

'Ordinary,' said Dover. The soggy biscuit was now sliding gently down the front of his pyjama jacket and his efforts to scoop it up were being hampered by the cigarette smoke that kept getting in his eyes.

MacGregor abandoned the voices. 'This taxi ride, sir, – how long would you say it was?'

'I wouldn't,' said Dover, always ready with the quick repartee. 'I could hardly consult my bloody watch, could I? Not with my eyes blindfolded.'

'Couldn't you make a guess, sir?'

'I dozed off, didn't I?' demanded Dover, getting cross. 'I'd had a hard day and it was dark and what with that bag thing pulled over my head ... The journey could have lasted five minutes or five hours for all I know.'

MacGregor had got a whole batch of questions about turning corners and stopping for traffic lights and speeding in a straight line down motorways. He now proceeded to forget about them and moved on to other topics. 'When you finally stopped, sir, did you get the impression that you were in a town or in the country?'

Dover looked at him in astonishment. 'How the hell should I know?'

'Didn't you hear anything, sir?'

'Such as what?'

'Well, cars and lorries going past, sir. Or owls hooting or cows mooing. Anything like that.'

Dover gazed blankly round the room. 'They ought to be bringing me my dinner soon.'

But MacGregor was not to be deflected from his purpose – and men have been given medals for less. 'Now, this "building" you say you were taken into, sir ...'

'Frog-marched!' Dover corrected him indignantly. 'My

37

arms are black and blue !'

'Was it a house, sir ?'

'What else could it have been, for God's sake ?'

'Well, it could have been a disused factory or a barn or a cricket pavilion or ...'

Dover blew unpleasantly down his nose. 'You've been seeing too many of these television thrillers, sonnie,' he observed scathingly. 'It was a house. *And* we went down a bit of a hall before we got to the stairs.'

That was better! MacGregor struck while the iron was tepid. 'Carpeted, sir ?'

Dover pondered long and hard over this one. Finally he shook his head. 'Bare boards!' he announced with somewhat unjustified pride. 'Stairs and hall!'

'Did you hear any aeroplanes flying overhead, sir ?'

Dover, not having seen the film in which this clue led to the capture of a whole clutch of kidnappers, was puzzled. 'Fat chance I had of hearing anything with that bloody row going on,' he grunted.

'What row, sir ?'

'The wireless, of course! Bloody pop music from morning till night. You must be tone deaf to listen to that sort of muck.'

MacGregor felt that he ought to cherish this unsolicited snippet of information so he wrote it down in full in his notebook. What did it mean, though ? That Dover's abductors were a bunch of raving teeny-boppers? Or were the Claret Tappers merely seeking for an effective way of drowning their victim's cries for help ?

''Strewth,' said Dover, smacking his lips, 'but this is thirsty work !'

MacGregor didn't fancy bearding the tea-lady again but he had at least to make the offer. 'Do you want some more coffee, sir ?'

'I was thinking more of a drop of the hard stuff,' said Dover with a grin.

'Sorry, sir,' – MacGregor managed to look as though he was

speaking the honest-to-God truth – 'but the doctor made a special point about that. Alcohol in any form would be absolutely fatal for you. It's something to do,' he added, shamelessly, 'with the drugs they've given you. Now,' – he ruffled the pages of his notebook – 'can you give me a few more details about this small room you were shut up in? How big was it, do you think? As big as this room? Half as big?'

'About that,' allowed Dover sulkily. He was still staggering from the body blow about the booze.

'Had it got a carpet?'

'No. The floor was covered with those square plastic tile things. Speckled brown.'

'What was the furniture like?'

Dover wriggled uneasily. 'There wasn't any. Well, apart from a pile of old army blankets on the floor where I was expected to sleep.'

'Were the walls papered or distempered?'

''Strewth!' Dover's fidgeting increased. 'Painted, I think. Cream.'

'I see,' said MacGregor encouragingly. 'Now, what about the fittings?'

'What fittings?' demanded Dover. 'Here,' – he put the kidnapping out of his mind and began excavating frantically under the bedclothes – 'where's my bloody bell?'

'Is this it, sir?' MacGregor hauled in a length of flex which had dropped down behind Dover's locker. 'Do you want me to ring it for you?'

'Three times!' gasped Dover. 'Quick, man!'

'Three times, sir?'

'For a bed-pan! Oh, get a bloody move on!' he howled as MacGregor's fingers seemed to falter. 'Don't be all day about it!'

Somewhat to Dover's surprise, MacGregor declined an invitation to remain and carry on with the interview. He covered his squeamishness by saying that he would take advantage of the short break to put in a phone call to the Yard and see if there

39

were any fresh developments. There weren't, of course, and MacGregor arrived back at the door of Dover's room as a boot-faced nurse emerged with a towel-draped utensil in her hand.

'All right for me to go back in now?' asked MacGregor brightly, keeping his eyes firmly fixed on the nurse's face.

The nurse responded with an indignant sniff. 'I suppose you know there is absolutely nothing to prevent that disgusting old brute in there from getting up and using the toilet at the end of the corridor?'

'Well,' said MacGregor somewhat uncertainly.

But the nurse wasn't waiting for an answer. Turning on her heel she marched furiously away.

MacGregor took up his role of inquisitor again. 'Have you remembered why the taxi looked wrong when you got in it, sir?'

Dover was trapped by the sharpness of the question into making a helpful answer. 'There was no chart thing stuck up by the meter telling you how much the bloody fare's gone up since last week. Bloody inflation!' He forestalled MacGregor's attempt to put another query. 'And the whole thing looked a bit battered and scruffy. Old, you know.'

MacGregor nodded. 'Sounds like a second-hand one, doesn't it, sir? Students, perhaps? There was quite a vogue for university students to drive around in old taxis a few years go. You didn't notice the registration number, did you, sir?'

'You must be joking!'

MacGregor would have liked to point out that he'd very little sense of humour left these days, but he didn't. Instead he returned to Dover's imprisonment in the house with the small room and the uncarpeted stairs. 'Now, the kidnappers held you, sir, from some time late on Tuesday night to early Thursday morning.'

Dover grunted his agreement. 'And it was a traumatic experience, laddie!'

'Were you kept in the same room all the time?'

'Never left it!' declared Dover proudly.

'When did they take your warrant card off you?'

Dover frowned. 'I didn't know they had.'

'They sent it with the ransom note, sir, as proof that they'd got you.'

Dover shrugged his shoulders. 'Must have dropped out of my pocket in the struggle,' he said indifferently. 'Cheeky devils!'

'What about food, sir?'

Dover perked up. 'Is it lunch-time already?'

MacGregor gritted his teeth. 'I meant when you were in the Claret Tappers' hands, sir.'

'Oh,' – Dover slumped back amongst his pillows – 'well, it was pretty lousy on the whole and there wasn't much of it.'

'They fed you in the room, did they, sir?'

'Two of 'em. One unlocked the door and held the gun on me while the other shoved a tray in on the floor. Like feeding time at the bloody zoo! And it's no good asking me if I saw their faces because they'd got scarves or balaclavas or something over their heads. And they went through the same sort of routine when they collected the tray.'

'Did they speak?'

Dover shook his head. 'Just growled "Get back!" at me or something like that.'

'What about when they released you, sir? Didn't they explain then what was happening?'

Dover sighed. He was getting bored with all this talk. 'No! They just came in, woke me up and said, "Come on!" – so I did. And so would you if you'd got a bloody gun pointing at your guts!'

'They put the bag on your head, sir, and tied you up?'

'Yes, and gagged me.' Dover straightened his top sheet and yawned. 'I'll make them rue the day they were born when I catch up with 'em.'

'Were you transported in the taxi again, sir?'

'Suppose so. Couldn't see, could I?'

41

'And you've no idea how long this journey took, either?'

From under dandruff-flecked eyebrows Dover glanced suspiciously at MacGregor. The young whippersnapper wasn't bloody well presuming to criticise, was he? 'I happened to be suffering from nervous exhaustion,' he said with some dignity.

'It must have been a very trying experience, sir,' said MacGregor, anxious to keep on the right side of the old fool for a bit longer. 'Did they put you in the big plastic bag in the taxi?'

'They made me climb into it out on the pavement,' answered Dover, quivering indignantly at the memory. 'Then they tied it tight round my neck. Trussed me up like a bloody chicken.'

'You didn't know you were dumped outside the Old Bailey, sir?'

'Think I'm flipping clairvoyant or something?' demanded Dover irritably. 'And now, that's enough! If you've got any more bleeding questions you'll have to keep 'em till this afternoon. Late this afternoon! The doctor said I had to have a nap after my lunch.'

'I've only got a couple more, sir,' said MacGregor. 'If you could just bear with me I needn't trouble you at all this afternoon.'

MacGregor decided to take the surly grunt as a sign of acquiescence. 'Now, this room you slept in ... this room you were kept in – it had an electric light switch? What shape was it? Round, flat? And the colour? What colour ...'

'It was square and white,' said Dover.

'And the electric light fitting, itself, sir?'

'God help us!' snarled Dover. 'A sort of shallow white bowl flat up on the ceiling.'

MacGregor could see that Dover's tolerance was wearing thin. 'What did you do about washing, sir?' he asked hurriedly. 'Did they take you to a bathroom or ...?'

'No,' said Dover.

'No, sir?'

'Strewth,' rumbled Dover. 'I was only there thirty-six hours. It doesn't do you any harm, you know, to go without a bloody

42

bath for thirty-six hours.'

'But sir,' objected MacGregor with a silly laugh, 'they must have let you go to the - er - the toilet. What . . . ?'

'You've had your quota!' roared Dover, plunging beneath the bedclothes and dragging the sheets up over his head. 'You said a couple of questions and you've asked about three hundred!'

Even MacGregor could see that Dover was trying to hide something. Greatly daring he pulled the sheet back from the chief inspector's face. 'Sir, you might be able to go thirty-six hours without washing but you can't go thirty-six hours without . . .' He caught Dover's irate and bloodshot gaze. 'Well, can you, sir?' he concluded weakly.

Dover suspected that if he didn't produce a satisfactory answer he wasn't going to be left alone in peace and quiet. Being a man of limited imagination he was often forced to fall back on the truth and that was the situation in which he found himself now. He glared miserably at his sergeant. 'I was *in* the lavatory, you bloody fool!' he hissed. 'That's where they kept me.'

'Oh,' said MacGregor, inadequately. 'Oh, I see.' He kept his voice nice and steady. It would never do to let Dover think that you found his predicament even remotely funny. 'Yes, well, quite a good idea really, sir. When you come to think about it. That's why there was no window, I suppose. Was there by any chance a ventilator?'

'Listen,' said Dover hoarsely. He leaned forward and gripped MacGregor by the lapels, pulling him too close for comfort. 'Listen! If you breathe a word about me being locked in the lavatory to anybody at the Yard - or anywhere else for that matter - I'll break every bleeding bone in your miserable body! Got it, laddie?'

MacGregor unhooked the clutching fingers. 'Yes, sir,' he said meekly. 'I've got it.'

Four

It was on the following morning that Chief Inspector Dover got his first taste of what it was like to be a celebrity. It happened just as he was being extricated by the combined efforts of MacGregor and the driver from the police car which had brought him to Paddington Station. A young woman, festooned with cockle-shells and draped in a horse-blanket, came rushing up. 'Ooooh!' she shrieked in wild delight. 'Ooooh, I know you!'

Dover was trying to get his breath back. 'Shove off!' he advised.

It is doubtful if the young woman even heard him. 'I know that face!' she squealed. 'I know it as well as my own!' She patted Dover's cheek affectionately. 'Little chubby chops, eh?'

Dover turned to MacGregor. 'Get rid of her!'

The young woman appealed to Paddington Station at large. 'Isn't he a scream?' She examined Dover more closely. 'I've seen you on the telly, haven't I? Now, what was it you were in? No, no,' - she gesticulated frantically in an effort to forestall assistance that was not actually forthcoming - 'don't tell me! It's on the tip of my tongue.'

44

'Don't just stand there, you damned fool!' howled Dover, venting his wrath as usual on his sergeant. 'Call a policeman!'

The young woman clung to Dover's arm. 'Was it "Dad's Army"?' she queried, creasing her forehead in what might have been thought. 'Or "My Old Man"?'

'Get your hands off me!' bawled Dover, attempting to get away but only succeeding in dragging the girl along with him. 'Leggo!'

'Here,' the young woman was having second - and nastier - thoughts 'you're not one of them politicians, are you?'

Dover and MacGregor were both big men and their combined strength finally broke the young woman's hold, though not her spirit. While MacGregor restrained her she fired one last shot in the direction of Dover's rapidly retreating back. 'You're the new Archbishop of Canterbury, aren't you? You see, I told you I'd get it - given time!'

'Silly cow,' said Dover when, a few minutes later, a somewhat dishevelled MacGregor joined him on the platform. 'Have you bought all the newspapers?'

Silently MacGregor displayed his bundle.

'Come on, then!' urged Dover impatiently. 'Let's find a seat. All this bloody standing around's doing me no good at all. I should be in bed by rights, you know. Or at least on a couple of weeks' sick leave. They've no business sending me off all over the country on a wild goose chase.'

They were walking along the platform, looking in the carriage windows.

'The train looks as though it's going to be rather full, sir.'

'Dartmoor!' scoffed Dover, already beginning to lag behind. 'It's a waste of time. That convict won't tell us a blind thing. You know it and I know it and ... Oh, 'strewth, let's get in here!'

'I'm afraid all the seats are booked, sir,' said MacGregor, turning to lug Dover up the step. 'We seem to have picked a rather popular train.'

'Booked?' Dover pushed his way into the carriage and surveyed the forest of tickets hanging down from the backs of the seats. 'We'll soon fix that!' He selected a couple of likely looking window seats and, leaning across, quickly ripped the reservation tickets off them. 'Here,' he commanded, pushing the tickets into MacGregor's nerveless hand, 'shove these in your pocket!'

'But, sir, we can't ... '

Dover was already inserting his seventeen and a quarter stone behind the little table. 'And, if anybody starts asking awkward questions, show 'em your warrant card and threaten to run 'em in if they don't belt up!'

There was trouble, of course, and MacGregor had to deal with it while Dover buried his head in his newspapers. There were complaints, appeals to MacGregor's sense of decency and finer feelings. The guard was fetched. Names and addresses were demanded and taken. In the end it didn't add up to much and that nice couple who were going to celebrate their golden wedding in Torquay still had to stand nearly all the way to Exeter.

Dover dropped the last newspaper to join the others in an untidy and disintegrating heap on the floor. He was very disappointed and, if he'd had a classical education, the adage *sic transit gloria mundi* might have come to mind. What on Wednesday had been: 'POLICEMAN! TRAGIC PAWN IN POLITICAL KIDNAPPING!' and on Thursday had been: 'WILF DOVER! SACRIFICIAL VICTIM IN TERROR SNATCH!' had now, on Friday morning, become half a column in the centre pages headed 'Lucky Jack Released Unharmed'.

'They haven't even put a picture of me in today,' whined Dover. 'That's all the thanks you get for laying down your life for your country!'

'Sir?'

Dover took violent exception to the quizzical way MacGregor raised his eyebrows. 'You just want to watch it, laddie!' he snarled. 'I was the one with his neck on the chopping block and don't you forget it! Nobody asked me if I minded being led like a lamb to the slaughter. You just wait till the next poor bugger has to face sudden death and see what he bloody well feels about it!'

MacGregor fancied he'd caught the faint whiff of a clue. 'You think the Claret Tappers will try again, sir?'

'Wouldn't you? 'Strewth, they still want the money and they still want their murderous chums out of the nick, don't they? I keep telling you, we're dealing with a bunch of blood-thirsty desperadoes and you'd do well to remember it.'

MacGregor leaned across the table as some of the most beautiful country in England raced unseen past the windows. 'Did you overhear them talking about doing a second kidnapping, sir?'

'You never stop, do you?' asked Dover wearily. 'I've told you a million times – I never heard 'em talking about anything. Why don't you wash your ears out?'

MacGregor sank back. Oh well, he might have guessed. He could see that Dover's eyelids were beginning to droop but there was no time to waste. The two hairy young men in walking boots who were occupying the seats next to the detectives had departed to the restaurant car but they would be back before long and their presence would put paid to any discussion of the case. Dover was just going to have to wait for his forty winks.

'I've been wondering, sir, if we might work on the assumption that the Claret Tappers are a London-based gang. Just a tentative hypothesis, you understand.'

Dover merely stared.

'I've been trying,' said MacGregor earnestly, 'to kind of *think* myself into the minds of the kidnappers.'

Dover's lips barely moved. 'God flipping help us!'

MacGregor pressed on. After all, the last thing he expected from his chief inspector was appreciation. 'I can't help feeling that the whole kidnapping was based in London, if you follow me. You were snatched in London, the ransom letter was

47

posted in London, they used a typical London taxi for transport and you were released in London. Now, as I figure it, all this must imply that we're looking for people who live in London or at least know the metropolis pretty well.'

Dover's piggy little eyes narrowed. 'If the whole caboodle's based in London,' he demanded crossly, 'what the blue blazes are we doing haring off to bloody Devon?'

The real reason for this tedious journey was the fact that Commander Brockhurst had reverted abruptly to his habitual policy of keeping Dover as far away from New Scotland Yard as was humanly possible. The moment he had heard that Dover was out of hospital and, in the opinion of his doctors, not only fit for duty but in dire need of it, he had started looking around for some way of getting rid of him. A visit to the distant Dartmoor Prison seemed a heaven-sent solution. 'And there's no need to hurry back,' he'd told MacGregor. 'I'd sooner have the job done properly than done badly in a sweat.'

Naturally MacGregor had to find a more diplomatic explanation than the crude truth for Dover. 'We have to see this Archibald Gallagher, sir. He's one of the men, if you remember, that the Claret Tappers wanted released from prison.'

'He'll not tell us anything,' grunted Dover. 'They never do. They take an oath or something. How much did he get, anyhow?'

'He got sentenced to eight years, sir.'

Dover's eyes opened wide. 'Eight years? 'Strewth, is that all? They should have given him life! If I had my way,' he added, turning his coat collar up and trying to burrow down inside it, 'I'd blow 'em up with their own bloody bombs.'

'We don't know that he'd anything to do with bombs, actually, sir.'

Dover didn't care for being contradicted but, thinking he'd found a way to stop MacGregor disturbing him, he let it go and sank even deeper into his greatcoat. 'Read me out what's-his-name's file, laddie!' he commanded. 'All of it, from cover to

48

cover.'

MacGregor saw through this ruse easily enough. Dover had, after all, used it countless times before. Well, it wasn't going to work on this occasion. 'I'm sorry, sir, but we haven't got a file on him.'

'Why not?'

'There's a go-slow in the Criminal Record Office, sir. They're working to rule or something. Anyhow, whatever it is, it's taking about a week to get a file out of them. It's only because I happen to have a friend working there that I was able to get what bit of information I have about Gallagher. At least we know what prison he's in.'

'Gallagher?' said Dover, looking anxious. 'That's an Irish name, isn't it?'

'It could be, sir,' agreed MacGregor.

Of recent years Dover had taken to seeing Greens rather than Reds under the bed and tended to get a trifle hysterical at any mention of the Emerald Isle. 'I should have known that lot were behind it!' he moaned.

'But none of your kidnappers were Irish, were they, sir? They didn't speak with Irish accents, did they?'

'They could have disguised them, couldn't they, you blockhead?' Dover glanced nervously round the railway carriage. The trouble was that everybody under twenty-five looked like a bloody anarchist these days. 'How long before we get there?'

'Oh, an hour or more, sir. There'll be a car waiting for us at ... '

'You keep your eyes skinned, then! I'm just going to have a bit of a quiet think.' Dover wriggled about to get comfortable. 'Don't you go dozing off, mind!'

'I won't, sir,' said MacGregor who had learnt to know when he was beaten. 'Er – will you want a cup of coffee if they come round with it?'

'Might as well,' said Dover. 'And get me a couple of sandwiches, too. Just to keep me going till lunch-time.'

49

The Deputy Governor kindly laid on a late lunch for them and was even rather pleased to see Dover scoff down everything edible in sight. 'I do like to see a man with a healthy appetite,' he said with an approving chuckle.

Dover mopped up the last crumbs of his ginger pudding and spooned half the contents of the sugar bowl into his coffee. He belched happily, undid the top button of his trousers and awarded his rosette. 'Not bad for prison grub.'

The Deputy Governor was modestly gratified. 'We've got a very good cook at the moment.'

MacGregor looked up. 'A prisoner, sir?'

'Oh, yes. A trusty, of course. A very decent chap. He's doing life for poisoning his mother-in-law but he's never given us a moment's anxiety.'

Dover was looking round expectantly. 'Somebody going to pass the fags round, eh?'

'Fags? Oh.' – the Deputy Governor's hospitable face fell – 'I'm afraid I don't smoke.'

'Well, nobody's perfect,' said Dover generously and turned to MacGregor.

Her Majesty's Prison Service didn't run to brandy, either, and Dover's instant and obvious displeasure cast a cloud over what had otherwise been a most delightful lunch.

MacGregor tried to cover things up by engaging the Deputy Governor in small talk. 'Er – what sort of a man is this chap Gallagher, sir?'

'Gallagher?' The Deputy Governor tore his eyes away from Dover's sullen face and made an effort to gather his thoughts. 'Oh, a very decent chap, you know. No trouble. I think you'll find him quite cooperative.'

'He'd better be!' Dover chipped in menacingly. He flourished a clenched and podgy fist. 'I've got the cure right here if he isn't!'

There being limits to how much even near saints like the Deputy Governor can stomach, Dover and MacGregor found themselves being shown out almost before they knew what was happening. They were conducted down long, apparently endless corridors with much locking and unlocking of heavy clanging doors. At the door of the room in which they were going to interview Archibald Gallagher, the Deputy Governor took a frosty-faced leave of them. 'Just ring for the prison officer when you've finished,' he asked, brushing aside MacGregor's attempts to thank him for his hospitality. 'He'll see you out.'

'Lah-di-dah poof!' muttered Dover, pushing his way into the interview room and flopping down on the nearest chair. ''Strewth, me feet aren't half giving me the old jip!'

MacGregor shouldered the burden of the interview so that Dover was left free to scrutinise the victim's demeanour or have a quiet kip as the fancy took him. 'You are Archibald Gallagher?'

The man lounging easily on the other side of the table wasn't most people's idea of a long-term convict and he fell a long way short of Dover's mental picture of a black-hearted, bloody-handed terrorist. With courteous charm he corrected MacGregor. 'Archibald St John Roderick Gallagher, actually.' He smiled. 'But you can call me Archie.'

MacGregor didn't care for being patronised by an old lag, however aristocratic his bearing or posh his accent. 'We're police officers,' he said, very po-faced.

Archibald St John Roderick Gallagher's smile widened. 'I would never have guessed!'

'I am Detective Sergeant MacGregor and this is ... '

'And this is Detective Chief Inspector Dover of the Murder Squad at New Scotland Yard!' Archie Gallagher's smile now ripened into a positive beam and, half rising to his feet, he reached across the table, seized Dover's hand and shook it warmly. 'I am delighted to make your acquaintance, sir! And may I congratulate you on your safe delivery from the clutches of those villains!'

Dover's jaw dropped and even MacGregor looked more than a little put out.

51

'You know Chief Inspector Dover?'

'Doesn't everybody, sergeant? The story of his kidnapping was carried as the lead in all the media, you know. Here in the nick it caused quite a deal of discussion. Some of my colleagues, I'm afraid, were slightly less than concerned about Mr Dover's fate.'

'I've put too many of 'em inside, that's why!' boasted Dover, recovering his aplomb. 'The underworld has no cause to love me.'

'Er – quite.' Archie Gallagher caught MacGregor's eye and winked.

MacGregor was not amused. It was one thing for Dover's fellow coppers to have a quiet snigger at the old fool behind his back but quite another to have a lousy convict trying to make a laughing stock out of him. 'In that case, Gallagher,' he said tartly, 'you'll understand why we're here.'

'Why should I, my dear fellow?'

'Oh, come off it!'

'No, really!'

MacGregor's eyes narrowed. 'Don't mess me about, chummy!'

'Scout's honour, sergeant!' Archie Gallagher's sense of humour was showing again. 'I've been racking my brains ever since they told me a couple of bogies were coming all the way from the Smoke especially to see me.' His eyes twinkled. 'I did think you might be bringing me the Queen's Pardon or something, but I can see it isn't that.'

MacGregor let him have it straight. 'We have reason to believe that you are connected with the Claret Tappers, the gang who kidnapped Chief Inspector Dover.'

'Me? Mixed up with a gang of kidnappers?' Archie Gallagher's laugh was highly infectious but there wasn't a flicker on MacGregor's face as he stared at the elegant convict. 'Is this your idea of a joke, sergeant?'

'Look,' said MacGregor in a bored voice, 'why don't you just come clean and save my time and yours?'

52

Archie Gallagher's manner changed. 'Save *my* time, cop- per?' he jeered. 'Time's the last thing I'm short of! I've got all the time in the world. Another five, goddam years in this stinking cess-pit so don't you talk to me about time! And besi- des' – he got his temper back under control – 'why should I do you lot any favours? The cops have never done anything for me.'

Dover bestirred himself to give a little fatherly advice to his sergeant. 'Slap him around a bit, laddie! Kick him in the kidneys! Shove your fist up his nose!'

'Hey! Watch it!' Archie Gallagher's composure slipped a little and, while actually speaking to Dover, he managed to keep a wary eye on MacGregor. 'He wouldn't dare!'

'Ho, wouldn't he? He may look a right little milk-sop but he's like a raving lion when he's roused.' Dover, as usual, was coming it a bit strong. 'And I'll swear you attacked him first,' he added shrewdly.

'Oh, sir!' wailed MacGregor. He found all this crude, boot- in-the-guts stuff not only distressing but humiliating.

'Well, get a move on then, for God's sake!' snarled Dover, throwing himself back petulantly in his chair. ''Strewth, I'm blowed if I'd let a blooming urban guerilla make a monkey out of me!'

There was no time for anybody to appreciate the joke.

'Urban guerilla?' repeated Archie Gallagher incredulously. 'What the hell are you talking about?'

A tiny worm of suspicion began to gnaw at MacGregor's mind. 'You are in here for terrorism, aren't you?' he asked. 'Planting bombs or organising riots or something in that line?'

Even hardened criminals have their pride. 'I am not!' roared Archie Gallagher indignantly. 'How dare you? I'm a multiple bigamist, for God's sake! I thought everybody knew that. As a matter of fact, I happen to disapprove very strongly of people employing violence to further their political ends.'

A pregnant silence followed this announcement.

'Well, gentlemen?'

MacGregor avoided looking at Archie Gallagher. 'When the kidnappers stipulated your release from prison as one of the conditions for freeing Chief Inspector Dover unharmed, we naturally – er – assumed that you were one of them. Or at least that you were in sympathy with their ideas.'

'Well, I'm not! Far from it! Ask anybody!'

Dover stuck his oar in. 'You've got an Irish name!'

'What's that got to do with it?'

'So you've probably got Irish sympathies!' Dover was never one to abandon a pet theory just because it was wrong.

Archie Gallagher was a gentleman and he broke the news as tactfully as he could. After all, in his profession you never knew when you might need a friendly policeman. 'Mr Dover, I had an Irish great grandfather. That's where the name comes from and that is my sole connection with Ireland, North or South. I've never even set foot in the place. Indeed, I pride myself that never, in my entire life, have I been further west than Torquay or further north than Cheltenham. You must understand that there's no scope for a man like me in Ireland.'

It didn't take much to get Dover's mind flying off at a tangent. 'How d'you mean,' he asked, 'no scope?'

Most people love talking about themselves and Archie Gallagher was no exception. To MacGregor's dismay, the two men settled down for a cosy chat.

'What outsiders don't seem to appreciate, my dear chap,' said Archie Gallagher, speaking with the voice of authority, 'is that bigamy is a profession, not a hobby. Getting rich women to the altar is deuced hard work, believe you me. Especially these days.'

'Harder now, is it?' asked Dover with a surprising show of sympathy.

'It's this permissive society, Mr Dover,' explained Archie Gallagher, shaking his head sadly. 'If you knew the difficulty of explaining to these dratted women why you want to *marry* them. They just can't understand why the blazes you should want to bother. When I first started, it was wedding bells or nothing, you know, but nowadays ... I'm talking about society women, of course. I don't have anything to do with the other sort. Oh, dear me, no! I came unstuck at the Horse Trials at Badminton, you know.' Archie Gallagher examined his immaculate fingernails with some pride. 'The arresting officer marched me right past Her Majesty. Ah me,' – he sighed deeply – 'it makes you wonder what the world's coming to.'

The disastrous decline of social standards since the halcyon days of his youth was a theme guaranteed to pluck at Dover's heart-strings. He positively beamed at Archie Gallagher. A kindred soul at last! In an excess of generosity Dover turned to MacGregor. 'Get your fags out, laddie!' he ordered imperiously. 'And hand 'em round! Do you smoke, Mr Gallagher?'

'Yes, but' – Archie Gallagher saw the colour of MacGregor's packet – 'not those, I'm afraid.' He extracted a slim box of fifty from the breast pocket of his prison battle-dress. 'Here, try one of mine!'

Dover accepted an expensive, hand-rolled, *emperor*-sized cigarette with great pleasure and almost indecent haste.

When he had provided a light all round, Archie Gallagher slipped his solid gold lighter back in his pocket. 'Yes,' he said, resuming the conversation where they had left off, 'bigamy is far from being the soft option some people fancy it is. And rich women are unbelievably mean, you know, and suspicious. Still,' – he smiled apologetically – 'I mustn't bore you with my troubles.'

Dover was not to be outdone in graciousness, not with cigarettes like Archie Gallagher's around. 'You're not boring us, old man! Is he, MacGregor?'

MacGregor managed a bit of a smile. 'How long have you been in prison, Gallagher?'

'This time? Eleven months, three days and about six hours.'

'So you've got the best part of seven years still to do?'

'Mr Justice Longbotham, in a most eloquent and moving speech, expressed the opinion that he owed it to society to make an example of me. He called me a heartless monster preying upon innocent women and regretted that he couldn't give me an even stiffer sentence. However, seven years is rather an exaggeration, sergeant. I expect to get quite a handsome remission for good behaviour.'

'With a box of fifty hand-made cigarettes in your pocket?' enquired MacGregor incredulously. 'I'll bet you've got a finger in every fiddle and racket there is going. You're damned lucky not to have lost your remission already!'

Archie Gallagher smiled. 'One counts on a modicum of luck,' he pointed out gently.

MacGregor tapped his teeth with the end of his pencil. 'I might be able to do something for you, Gallagher,' he said.

'Like guarantee me my remission?' Archie Gallagher's smile was mocking.

'Or there's parole. A word in the right place from us ...'

'And what, sergeant, do I have to do to earn a place in your good books?'

Dover got it in first. 'How about handing your fags round again?'

Archie Gallagher was a generous man. 'Here,' he said, handing the box over, 'take the lot! I can get plenty more.'

'Oh, ta!' said Dover, wondering if there was any chance of getting the gold lighter as a little souvenir of their meeting.

MacGregor attempted to get the interview back under his control. 'You play ball with us,' he told Gallagher, 'and we'll play ball with you!'

'But I've already told you, I don't know anything.'

MacGregor watched Gallagher carefully. 'You've never heard of the Claret Tappers?'

'Never.'

'They're the bastards who kidnapped *me* in order to get *you* out of the nick,' grumbled Dover, lest anybody should forget that he'd got a grievance.

'Are you sure you've never heard of them?'

'Quite sure, sergeant! Believe me, I'd help you if I could.'

'Have you any suggestions, though?' appealed MacGregor.

56

'Doesn't any of this mean anything to you?'

Archie Gallagher shrugged his shoulders. 'Well, it sounds terribly far fetched but, honestly, the only thing I can think of is that your Claret Tappers might possibly be Wykehamists.'

'Wykehamists?' The consternation on MacGregor's face might have been amusing if it hadn't been so obviously heartfelt. The sergeant had been educated at a very minor public school but he wasn't in this league. He gazed in awe at the urbane bigamist and cleared his throat. 'Were you at Winchester?' he asked in an envious croak.

Archie Gallagher chuckled. 'No,' he admitted without a trace of shame. 'But I always say I was. I always think a good educational background impresses people, don't you?'

Five

Dover raised a face crimson with exertion and dripping with foam. 'Ah, that's better!' he asserted happily and set his pint tankard down with a thump on the old, formica-top table.

MacGregor, ensconced opposite in the other antique plastic settle, responded with a feeble smile. 'Cheers, sir!' he said, sipping his glass of unadulterated tonic water without enthusiasm and finding scant comfort in the knowledge that one of the partnership at least would have a clear head for the afternoon.

'Best beer for five miles around!' claimed Dover. It wasn't true. The only reason the chief inspector patronised this rather dirty and inconvenient pub was that it was the sole establishment within reasonable range of Scotland Yard that wasn't haunted by hordes of thirsty policemen. Dover lived in the constant fear that one day he would be called upon to stand his round and so he took what precautions he could.

'A cigarette, sir?'

Dover accepted, but only under duress. 'I can't think why you don't buy yourself some decent fags,' he grumbled.

'These are all I can afford, sir.'

'That Gallagher chap must have made a packet out of

58

bigamy,' said Dover enviously. 'Talk about money for bloody jam!'

'It sounded more like the dickens of a lot of hard work, the way he told it, sir. And the risks! Why, he'd got six women at the end, all coming from more or less the same social stratum and all thinking they were married to him. No wonder it all came unstuck. I'd love to have been at Badminton, though, when Numbers Two and Five spotted him arming a prospective Number Seven around.' MacGregor took another mouthful of tonic. 'Serves him right for picking all his women from the horsey set.'

Dover dried off his moustache with the back of his hand. 'Horses? I thought you played badminton with a bat and one of those shuttlecock things.'

MacGregor had neither the strength nor the inclination to start teaching Dover the facts of sporting life and he changed the subject slightly, hoping that old bird-brain wouldn't notice. 'Did you believe Archie Gallagher, sir? About not being mixed up in any way with the Claret Tappers?'

'He seemed genuine enough,' said Dover, who'd developed quite a soft spot for the bigamist. 'Sounded as though he was telling the truth.'

'He is a professional liar, of course, sir. He makes his living by deceiving people.'

'Only a pack of silly women.'

MacGregor wasn't so sure. 'I imagine that yarn about being educated at Winchester must have fooled a number of men, too, sir. Or else why would he imagine that the Claret Tappers might be a bunch of old Wykehamists?'

Dover was even less *au fait* with the old school tie ethic than he was with sport. 'Well, he's not a terrorist, that's for sure.'

MacGregor sighed. 'No, I'm inclined to agree with you there, sir.'

'Ho, ta very much!'

MacGregor ground his teeth, but silently. 'Maybe we'll have more luck this afternoon with the other one.'

Dover stopped rattling his empty glass on the table. 'What other one?'

'The other prisoner, sir. The Claret Tappers demanded the release of two prisoners . . . if you remember.'

'So where've we got to go this afternoon?' whined Dover, beginning to panic at the mere prospect of work. 'Bloody north of Scotland?'

'Only to Holloway, sir.' MacGregor was relieved to be the bearer of good news for a change. 'And we can go by taxi. Commander Brockhurst said he would authorise it, just this once.'

'I saw old Brockhurst this morning,' said Dover gloomily. 'We travelled up in the same lift.'

'Really, sir?' Commander Brockhurst must be slowing up, thought MacGregor. He usually took good care not to let Dover get within spitting distance.

'He spoke to me,' said Dover.

MacGregor reckoned senile decay must be setting in. 'Er – what did he say, sir?'

Dover sagged like a partially deflated barrage balloon. 'Only "Good morning". I was just going to tell him exactly what I thought about the way my kidnapping was handled when we reached his floor and he got out.'

Never a dull moment, thought MacGregor.

'The whole thing's been a cock-up from the beginning, if you ask me,' said Dover. 'And now look what's happening! First I have to go rushing off to bloody Devon and now it's bloody Holloway. Is nobody else going to do anything? 'Strewth, they ought to be deploying every copper in the country to help nab these villains, not leaving it all to me. I mean, there's a limit to what one man can do – however bloody willing.'

'Several other lines of enquiry are being pursued, sir.'

Dover sniffed sceptically. 'Such as what?'

'Well, a nationwide search is being made for that taxi, sir, and they're following up every report from the general public

60

that might lead to the identification of the house in which you were detained. People are being extraordinarily helpful, sir.'

Dover dismissed all these public-spirited citizens with a rude gesture. 'Nut cases!'

'And of course, Special Branch are busy trying to pick up the trail of these Claret Tappers, sir. If they *are* a gang of terrorists, somebody somewhere must know something about them. And then...'

'All right, all right!' snarled Dover. 'There's no need to make a bloody meal of it!' His face brightened suddenly. 'And, talking of meals, how about bringing me back a few sandwiches and a couple of pies when you get me another beer?' His glass was pushed across the table. 'Not cheese. Cheese makes me bilious.'

MacGregor drained his own glass and stood up. In his more despairing moments he calculated that half his pay went to the upkeep of Dover's inner man. 'Would you like a bowl of soup to start with, sir?'

The trouble with sarcasm was that Dover never saw it. 'Might as well,' he said. 'Hey, hold your horses!' His anguished yelp stopped MacGregor in his tracks. 'Holloway? That's a women's prison!'

MacGregor nodded. 'That's right, sir. The second prisoner is a woman. Lesley Whittacker. Your Claret Tappers had her down as Les Whittacker and it took the C.R.O. a bit to identify her. She's doing two years for shop-lifting.'

More echoing corridors and clanging doors. This time, though, it was a woman prison officer who marched Dover and MacGregor along like a couple of defaulters.

The wardress may have looked as though she'd played Rugby League in her youth for England but, beneath that rugged exterior, there beat a heart of gold. She unlocked the door of the punishment cell which was to be used for the interview. Before she opened it she issued a word of warning. 'You'll have to watch her!'

MacGregor smiled. 'There are two of us,' he pointed out.

'Just as well, sergeant, because she'd make mincemeat of a young lad like you if she got you on your own. I'll be right outside if you need me but – take my advice – don't turn your back on her!' She flung the door open and stood aside to let the two detectives enter. As Dover lumbered past she caught him by the sleeve. 'Pardon me for mentioning it, dear, but have you ever thought of going on a diet?'

If she'd stripped off and done a belly dance, Dover's eyes couldn't have popped rounder than they did.

The woman prison officer shook her head over Dover's paunch. 'You do so remind me of my father,' she whispered sadly. 'He was stones and stones overweight, too.'

'But he went on a bloody diet, I suppose?' Dover was sick of being told about these paragons who stopped smoking or eating or what-have-you at the drop of a bleeding hat.

The woman prison officer's eyes had filled with tears. 'Oh, no, dear! He died. Went out like a light. And the trouble we had getting that coffin round the bend in the stairs, you wouldn't believe. It took all the paint off the banisters. So, do try and take some of that excess fat off, dear, if only for the sake of those you leave behind!'

Dover was not in the best of moods when he finally elbowed his way into the interview room. That damned female screw! She wanted punching up the hooter! He was so cross that it took him quite a few seconds before he began to register his surroundings. Then he realised that he was in a rather dark, small room with bare walls and a barred window set up high out of reach. The furnishings consisted of three wooden chairs grouped companionably round a small wooden table.

On one of the chairs a young woman was lounging. She looked as though she was about to fulfil America's manifest destiny by following the covered wagons towards the setting sun. The enveloping shawl and the ankle-length dress were, of course, part of the new dispensation by which women prisoners were allowed to wear their own gear while inside. Dover, it

62

need hardly be said, disapproved. In his book anybody stupid enough to get themselves nicked deserved an unrelieved regime of sackcloth, broad arrows and bread and water.

Miss Lesley Whittacker propelled her wodge of chewing gum from her right cheek to her left. 'Why do you bogies always go round in two's?' she asked.

MacGregor was too old a hand to get involved in that sort of question and answer session. He concentrated on introducing himself and Dover and on giving Miss Whittacker a brief résumé of the reasons for their visit.

Miss Whittacker was impressed. 'Fancy,' she said.

'We have been given to believe,' MacGregor continued smoothly, 'that you may be able to assist us in our enquiries.'

Miss Whittacker addressed herself to Dover. 'Ooh, doesn't he talk posh?' she asked admiringly. 'Not a bit like all the effing old pigs I've had to deal with.'

Dover responded with an admonition whose vocabulary, tone and accent were calculated to make Miss Whittacker feel much more at home.

'You old sod!' she chuckled. 'Actually, he hasn't asked me no bleeding questions yet, has he?'

'What do you know about the Claret Tappers?' demanded MacGregor.

'Not a sodding thing, duckie!'

'That's the name of the gang that kidnapped Chief Inspector Dover, here.'

'I've still never heard of 'em, but you can give 'em my heartiest congratulations when you catch up with 'em.'

MacGregor's voice hardened. 'Don't give me all that crap, girl! You're one of 'em, aren't you?'

'Me?' asked Miss Whittacker wearily. 'Come off it, Blue-eyes! Why should I go around kidnapping fat old policemen, for Christ's sake?'

'How about a hundred thousand pounds in ransom money?' snapped MacGregor.

Miss Whittacker merely laughed. 'Chance'd be a fine thing!

Look, copper, I've been shut up in this cat house for twelve bleeding months, haven't I? You tell me how I can be a part of a snatch for a hundred thousand nicker while I'm doing porridge and I'll oblige. Like an effing shot!'

Dover scowled at the girl. 'You've been in Holloway for the past year?'

'More or less.'

Dover's scowl deepened. 'And what the hell's that supposed to mean?'

'It means, pig,' spat Miss Whittacker, 'that they kept me hanging about for a couple of bleeding weeks in Bristol, didn't they?'

Dover had no scruples about hitting women, indeed on the whole he preferred it. There was less danger of retaliation. Before he'd got his clenched fist raised more than a couple of inches, though, MacGregor came galloping to the rescue with a penetrating and diversionary question.

'Why should the Claret Tappers stipulate that you should be released from prison?'

Lesley Whittacker shrugged her shoulders. Underneath all the draperies and a lot of rather amateurishly applied make-up there was quite a pretty girl. MacGregor was just beginning to notice. 'Search me,' she said.

MacGregor cleared his throat. 'Look, Lesley,' he said, switching to a more friendly approach, 'I know you really couldn't care less whether anybody kidnaps Mr Dover or not. I mean, no policeman's exactly your best friend, is he?'

'The lousy pigs!' said Miss Whittacker viciously. She snatched her chewing-gum out of her mouth and slapped it angrily on the underside of the table. 'I were fixed at Bristol, you know. First that bloody store detective swearing black was white so's she'd get her effing promotion and then that bleeding copper lying in his teeth. And they wouldn't let me telephone my solicitor, either. Talk about a put-up job! I ask you – what would I want with eight transistors and five stop watches, for God's sake?'

64

MacGregor could see that Dover was growing restless. 'Yes, rotten luck,' he said. 'But to get back to these Claret Tappers. We must catch them, you see, because they might try again and next time they might take somebody who wasn't a policeman.'

Miss Whittacker went slightly cross-eyed as she attempted to work this out but analytical thought was not her strong point. 'Well?'

'Well,' said MacGregor, sensing that he was on a hiding to nothing, 'well, I'm - er - sure you wouldn't want to see an innocent person hurt, would you?'

'I wouldn't mind,' said Miss Whittacker with massive indifference. 'I was innocent and look where it's landed me.'

'You got a boy friend, miss?'

Much to MacGregor's fury, Lesley Whittacker seemed to recognise her master's voice. Although she kept a wary eye on Dover, she answered his question promptly. 'I got dozens.'

'Politics?'

'I'm a Conservative. They're the ones with the yachts, you know, and the villas in the South of France and going shooting at Ascot and ...'

Dover, having got the whole problem well and truly licked, sat back. 'So, there's your answer!' he informed MacGregor.

'Sir?'

'' Strewth, do I have to spell every bloody thing out for you? Look, it's perfectly obvious what's happened.'

'Is it, sir?'

'If you'd keep your trap shut for a minute, I'd tell you!' snarled Dover. He gesticulated in the direction of the now open-mouthed Miss Whittacker. 'This girl's not one of your political agitators. Any fool can see that. And, if she's been shut up in the nick for the last twelve months, she can hardly have had a hand in my kidnapping, can she?'

'Well,' began MacGregor doubtfully.

But Dover was after a cup of tea and a couple of buns in the prison officers' sitting-room, not a bloody debating society session. 'So, if somebody wants to spring her, it's not for the sake of her vote at the next flaming general election, is it?'

'You think she's some kind of gangster's moll, sir?' asked MacGregor, being careful to keep the smirk off his face. 'One – or all, perhaps – of the Claret Tappers wanted her released on account of her – er – physical charms?'

Dover's face settled into a sullen pout. 'You got a better suggestion?'

Support for his theory came from an unexpected quarter. Miss Whittacker, it turned out, was for it one hundred per cent. Most of her day-dreams so far had been concerned with extremely large amounts of money, but she wasn't a complete stranger to sexual fantasies. After all, it wasn't such a big change as all that. She could still have the white sports cars and the jewels and the posh food and everything. The thought that somewhere there was a Master Criminal nursing an unrequited passion for her was heady stuff. She sat up straight, moistened her lips and threw her chest out.

MacGregor looked at her dubiously. 'Can you think of any of your boy friends who would go to such lengths?' he asked.

Miss Whittacker let her breath out. A *requited* passion? That was a possibility which had not crossed her mind. 'Maybe,' she said.

MacGregor glanced at Dover to see if he was expected to play this silly farce out to the bitter end. He was. With a suppressed sigh he turned to a clean page in his notebook. 'Perhaps you could let me have a few names?'

Miss Whittacker looked vacant. 'Names?'

'Of your boy friends. So that we can check them out and see if any of them could be involved in this kidnapping business.'

'Oh.' Miss Whittacker sagged a little. All that sort of thing seemed such a long time ago. Seemed? Jesus, it *was* a long time ago! 'Well,' – she groped about in the rag-bag of her memory – 'there was Sid and ... and Peter. Oh, and Black George. I shan't forget him in a bleeding hurry. Rotten swine! And he nicked my bloody rent money when he went! Sod him. Then there was Freddie – not that he was much better. And Tony.'

66

She broke off to consult MacGregor on a technical point. 'Do you count 'em if they couldn't quite bring it off, dear? I mean, you had to give Tony full marks for trying but ... '

'Let's forget about Tony,' said MacGregor hurriedly. 'What I would like, though, are a few names. We can't really start looking for people if all we know about them is that they're called Sid, can we?'

Miss Whittacker's face fell. 'Surnames?'

MacGregor could see what was coming. 'Even one or two would be a help.'

Miss Whittacker shook her head. 'I've got a shocking memory, you see.' She reached under the table and retrieved her chewing gum. 'Tony was called Jenkins – that I do know. But you say you're not interested in him.'

MacGregor sighed. 'Could he be one of the kidnappers, do you think?'

Miss Whittacker masticated slowly. 'Shouldn't think so, lovey. He went to Australia with his mum and dad three years ago and, as far as I know, he's still there.'

Dover was already on his feet. 'We're wasting our bloody time here,' he announced, giving the door a savage kick.

MacGregor closed his notebook and stood up, too. He smiled at Miss Whittacker. 'Well, thanks very much, anyhow. If you do think of anything that might help ... '

'Oh, I'll let you know all right, dear,' she promised as she sorted out her funereal draperies preparatory to taking her own departure.

'These any good to you?'

Miss Whittacker accepted the cigarettes gratefully. 'I can always do with a bit of extra snout. Ta!' The packet of cigarettes disappeared under a quantity of hand-knitted tatt that she was festooning round her shoulders. 'There's something else you could do for us.'

'What?' As a precautionary measure MacGregor moved nearer to the door through which Dover had already disappeared. Well, twelve months is a long time for a nubile young

67

woman to be shut up in ... Much to his relief the female prison officer appeared in the doorway and rattled her keys. 'What do you want?'

Miss Whittacker sidled closer. 'These kidnappers,' she whispered. 'You might let us know who they are if you ever find 'em.'

'Come on, Whittacker!' bawled the screw.

Miss Whittacker smiled up at MacGregor and even laid a provocative hand on his arm as she went past him. He decided later that this must have been when she pinched his cigarette lighter. 'I'd just like to know who he is – see? I mean, he must be pretty bloody hot stuff to go to all this trouble, mustn't he?' She drooped one mascara loaded eyelid. 'And Les doesn't stand for Lesbian, you know!'

It was MacGregor's day for receiving irrelevant confidences. Even the female wardress opened her heart to him, bending down so that she could whisper in his ear.

'Is your Mr Dover doing anything about his dandruff, sergeant? I happen to have a really most effective formula that I'm sure would clear it up for him in no time. If I sent it to you, care of Scotland Yard, would you undertake to see that he ... '

Having transported two cups of tea, a plate of sandwiches, a plate of cakes and a plate containing two sausage rolls and a pie from the café counter to the table, MacGregor pocketed the few coppers which had been handed to him in change and sat down.

'Sugar!'

MacGregor pushed the plastic sugar dispenser across the table and stared dejectedly into the depths of his own cup of tea. On the other side of the table Dover was shovelling food into his mouth with considerable gusto. Talk about feeding time at the zoo! 'Well, that didn't get us very far, did it, sir?'

'Could've told you that!'

MacGregor picked up his spoon and began to dredge out the flakes of sausage roll pastry which Dover's ejaculation had

68

blown into his tea. 'So where do we go from here, sir?'

'Dunno about you,' grunted Dover, 'but I'm going home!' This was apparently one of Dover's little jokes and he chuckled ecstatically over it.

MacGregor waited until the eruptions had subsided. 'Are we going to work on the assumption then, sir, that neither Whittacker nor Gallagher knows the identity of the Claret Tappers?'

'What else?' asked Dover, washing down most of the pie with a swig of tea. 'I told you they'd both turn out to be a dead loss. We'd have done better to stay in the office. It'd have been warmer, too,' he added sourly.

MacGregor took it upon himself to look on the bright side 'I don't think our trips were a complete wash-out, sir. After all, the kidnappers did mention those two specifically, by name. There must be a connection somewhere.'

'Why?' Dover's podgy paw was hovering over the last two cakes, trying to settle his order of precedence. 'It could all have been a joke. While the Claret Tappers were asking for the bloody moon, they reckoned they might as well chuck in a couple of crummy cons for good measure.' He gave the chocolate eclair his casting vote. 'So they picked our two beauties at random.'

MacGregor frowned. 'That won't do, sir.'

'Whawhanoo?'.

MacGregor responded to the spirit of the question. 'Well, you and I could probably produce the names of a number of convicts, sir, but I doubt if ordinary members of the public could.'

Dover licked the bits of chocolate off his moustache and reached for the shrinking maid of honour. 'The Claret Tappers are policemen?'

MacGregor bit his lip. God, it was like dealing with a gibbering idiot! 'There are other professions, sir, who might be familiar with the names of prisoners – lawyers, journalists, other prisoners, warders ...'

'And anybody bright enough to read a flaming newspaper!' snorted Dover. 'Which narrows the field down to about nine-tenths of the bloody population! What's to stop these Claret Tappers just picking up the nearest daily rag and sticking a pin in the reports of the court proceedings, eh? I sometimes wonder what you use instead of brains, laddie.'

'If that's all they did, sir,' objected MacGregor, stunned into defending himself, 'why didn't they land on somebody who was being tried and sentenced much more recently? Gallagher and Whittacker are a pretty un-newsworthy pair, sir, but, if their names ever did appear in the newspapers, it would have been at least a year ago. Are you suggesting that your kidnappers planned that sort of detail as much as twelve months ago?'

'Yes,' said Dover firmly. He'd had more than enough for one day. 'That's why you've got it all wrong as usual, laddie! There must be a connection but you're just not bright enough to see it. Anyhow, I'm not sitting here all day arguing the toss with you. Nip out and get a taxi and let's be getting home!'

'A taxi, sir?'

'You said old Brockhurst authorised one, didn't you, moron?'

There were some moments in his life with Dover that even MacGregor enjoyed. 'Ah,' he pointed out with a great deal of relish, 'but that was for *going* to Holloway, sir. The commander said nothing about having a taxi for the return journey.'

'In that case, sonnie,' sniggered Dover, confident that he could out-smart MacGregor with both hands tied behind his back, 'you'll have to foot the bill, won't you?'

Six

Whenever he was engaged on a case involving serious crime MacGregor adhered strictly to the best traditions of the C.I.D. and worked through at least the first seventy-two hours without a break. He fully appreciated how important speed was and how essential it was to make full use of the first few days after the perpetration of any crime. Every detective knows, to his sorrow, how quickly memories fade and clues get themselves erased.

Dover, on the other hand, had his own methods. Self educated in the 'more-haste-less-speed' school, he never did today what he could postpone to the middle of next week. In his spare time he was also a staunch supporter of the Lord's Day Observance Society and extraordinarily scrupulous in his acknowledgement of every holiday permitted by either church or state.

Nobody, therefore, was more surprised than MacGregor when the door of their office opened and the dejected figure of Detective Chief Inspector Dover shuffled in. 'Er – good morning, sir! I – er – wasn't expecting to see you at the Yard today.'

'Why not?' Dover, retaining his overcoat and bowler hat,

71

squeezed with some difficulty into the chair behind his desk. The room he was obliged to share with MacGregor was little more than a glorified broom cupboard and it was a tight fit when the two of them were there.

'Well, it's *Sunday*, actually, sir.'

'Very funny,' said Dover, mentally consigning all members of the opposite sex to endless torment and hell fire. Had it not been for his lady wife and so-called help-mate, he could have been spending the Sabbath where any red-blooded man ought to be spending it – in bed. The trouble was that Mrs Dover, having set her heart on spending the first few days of her widowhood with a married niece in Clacton, didn't see why she should change her plans just because an enigmatic Providence had dashed her fondest hopes. So Dover had reluctantly had to come in to work, there being no fun in staying at home without somebody to wait on you hand and foot. 'Watcherdoin?' he asked.

MacGregor gestured at several files which were spread out over his desk. 'I've just been going through these crank letters, sir, in the hope that I might be able to winnow out a little corn from all the chaff.'

Dover grunted. He didn't go much on these agricultural metaphors.

'Er – would you like to help, sir?'

Dover reacted as though MacGregor had made an improper suggestion to him – which, in a way, he had. 'Doing what?' he asked suspiciously.

'Well, I thought you might like to go through one of these files, sir. There's this one, for example.' MacGregor picked up the bulkiest file of the lot. 'These are all the letters we've had from members of the general public about suspicious taxi cabs.' MacGregor sighed and dropped the file back on his desk. 'It looks as if every lunatic in London has taken time off to drop us a line. That's the trouble with taxis. Everybody's seen them doing something cock-eyed at some time or other.'

Dover pointed a nicotined forefinger at a much slimmer file.

'How about that one?'

MacGregor read the title ' "Empty & Unfurnished Houses within Fifty Miles of Charing Cross", sir. These are from people who think they might have found the place where you were held captive. There's another file, "Empty & Unfurnished Houses over Fifty Miles from Charing Cross", but I didn't bother to bring that. We can't cover the entire country and, unless we get some positive ... '

'Gimme!'

'The "Empty & Unfurnished", sir?'

'What else?' Dover took the file and opened it out on his desk. Resting his head upon one hand, he flicked over a few of the enclosures. Gradually his movements became slower and slower until, finally, they stopped altogether.

MacGregor smiled superciliously to himself and settled down to sift through yet another file. Half an hour later he flung his pencil down in an agony of frustration and conceded that Dover had triumphed once again. That bloody snoring!

Dover gulped, snorted, smacked his lips, blew down his nose and opened one pink-rimmed eye. 'Huh?'

'Sorry, sir, I dropped my pencil.'

'Huh.'

MacGregor got in quick before the old pig dozed off again. 'I was thinking, sir. It might be a rather good idea if we sort of reconstructed the actual snatch. When the taxi picked you up, I mean.'

Dover yawned.

'I thought we might just go over the ground, sir, on the way to The Two Feathers, sir.'

Dover accepted the bribe of a pre-lunch drink with alacrity. He banged his unread file shut and shoved his desk back. 'Come on!' he said.

MacGregor, whom the moving of the furniture had shunted up against the far wall, was taken aback by the success of his ploy. 'But it's only ten o'clock, sir!'

'So we'll be first in the queue, laddie!'

73

The West End of London on a chilly Sunday morning in January is not a very densely populated place and there was, mercifully, no-one about as Dover and MacGregor emerged through the huge glass doors of New Scotland Yard. From the entrance hall an indifferent uniformed policeman on guard duty watched them pick their way down the shallow steps and then went back to worrying about his own problems.

'It's bloody cold!' complained Dover, shivering elaborately.

MacGregor had already taken a solemn vow that he was going to stick to his last, come what may. 'You set off down Broadway towards Victoria Street, didn't you, sir?'

'No,' snarled Dover, waxing sarcastic, 'I went *up* Broadway towards bloody Timbuktu!'

MacGregor silently counted up to ten. 'How far had you got, sir, when you noticed the taxi?'

Dover flapped a languid paw. ''Bout here.' Well, he'd walked far enough and what flaming difference did it make anyhow?

MacGregor nodded wisely. 'And the taxi came up behind you and overtook you, sir? Now, where precisely did it stop?'

Dover flapped another paw.

MacGregor nodded again. 'Just far enough to make it difficult for you to see in the dark who it was. Clever. Did the light inside the taxi come on when the door was opened, sir?'

'No.' Dover flapped his arms in an attempt to keep warm.

MacGregor forebore to make any comment. Nevertheless, the non-functioning courtesy light was a point which should have put a trained and experienced detective on his guard. MacGregor led the way to where the mystery taxi had purportedly pulled up and, narrow-eyed, surveyed the scene. 'And the third man approached from behind, sir, as you were standing here looking into the interior of the taxi?'

''Sright.' Dover blew violently into his cupped hands.

'He was probably lurking in the angle of the wall there, sir. It would be quite dark there at night because the street lighting wouldn't...'

74

'Are we going to be standing around here all blooming day?'
Dover stamped his feet.

MacGregor remained adamant. 'I'll come back later and
make a sketch map,' he conceded, 'but there are one or two
more points which really must be cleared up, sir.'

Bloody little Sherlock Holmes, thought Dover. 'Well?'

'You entered the taxi, sir ...'

'At gun point!'

'... and it drove off?'

'Yes!'

'Which way?'

'Towards Victoria Street, of course. The way it was facing.'

'Good, good!' MacGregor smiled encouragingly, much as
he would have done at a backward child. 'So, you go down
Broadway and reach Victoria Street. Then which way did you
go? Did you turn to the right or to the left?'

'I don't know,' replied Dover impatiently. 'I told you – soon
as I got in the taxi, they jumped me. They were swarming all
over me. I'd got enough to do without thinking which bloody
way we were turning.'

'Do you remember the cab stopping for the traffic lights,
sir?'

But Dover had had enough. His flabby jowls wobbled
crossly. 'I don't remember anything – and neither would you if
you'd been in my bloody shoes!'

MacGregor would have liked to dispute that assertion but he
didn't. He permitted himself a slight shrug and then gazed
around, seeking inspiration from the bleak grey sky which was
hanging over London. Not that he could see much sky. There
were buildings all around and the soaring façade of New Scotland Yard with its countless windows dominated the scene.
MacGregor shook his head. 'It's strange that nobody saw anything, sir. You'd have thought somebody in the Yard would
have been looking out of one of those windows at the right
time, wouldn't you?'

'It was dark,' grunted Dover. 'And I don't suppose it would

look all that suspicious from up there. Now, are we going?'

'Just a minute, sir!' Selflessly disregarding all the health hazards that were likely to ensue from contact with Dover's overcoat, MacGregor placed a restraining hand on his master's arm.

Dover, who had his own ideas about MacGregor's proclivities, shied away like a frightened horse. 'Hey, watch it!'

But MacGregor was too excited to register yet another slur on his manhood. 'Sir,' he said, still hanging onto Dover like grim death, 'we really should have thought of this before!'

'Thought of what?'

'How did the kidnappers know the exact time of your departure from the Yard?'

'They didn't.' If it meant taking the wind out of MacGregor's sails, Dover could think with surprising speed and logic. 'They just hovered around waiting till I appeared.'

MacGregor considered this and then firmly shook his head. 'No, that won't work, sir. Scotland Yard is a pretty sensitive area these days. Even a taxi couldn't hang around here for three hours without somebody getting suspicious. They're down on parked vehicles like a ton of bricks.'

'Who says it was parked?' asked Dover. 'They could have just driven round and round. Nobody'd pay any attention to a passing taxi.'

'But they might have missed you, sir. They could easily have been stuck in a traffic jam out in Victoria Street when you left the Yard. And suppose there'd been other policemen knocking about – would the Claret Tappers have risked abducting you from under the noses of a pack of trained observers? Or suppose you'd been with somebody? Me, for example. They could never have pulled off a stunt like that if I'd been with you.'

It took Dover a bit longer to pick holes in this argument. 'Maybe you *were* with me!'

MacGregor broke the news gently. 'I was on my Explosives Course, sir.'

This information was greeted with a really vicious scowl. 'I mean earlier on, you bloody fool. The Claret Tappers could have been waiting for the right opportunity for weeks for all we know. Maybe Tuesday was simply the first chance they had. There weren't any coppers around and I hadn't anybody with me. Anyhow,' – he sniffed loudly – 'what was all that about three hours?'

'Three . . . ? Oh, well, just that normally, sir, you leave the Yard at five o'clock. If not earlier. If the kidnappers were counting on you keeping to your usual routine on Tuesday, they would have had to wait, hanging around, for three hours. It doesn't sound very likely, sir, does it?'

Dover's bottom lip stuck out. 'It was old Brockhurst,' he explained sulkily. 'While you were away, the rat took to ringing me up just before knocking off time. Trying to catch me out, you see, in case I left early.'

It was MacGregor's turn to start feeling cold. There was a biting gale whistling down the street. 'I don't quite see what you're getting at, sir.'

'The kidnappers wouldn't have had to wait three hours for me to come out of the Yard on Tuesday,' explained Dover with remarkable patience. 'They would only have had to wait two because, thanks to old Brockhurst, I had to sit there twiddling my bloody thumbs till six.'

'Does it really make all that much difference, sir?' asked MacGregor. 'The taxi wouldn't have hung around for two hours any more than for three.'

'I was just trying to keep the record straight,' said Dover. 'And now, if you've finished, let's get to the boozer. It's cold enough out here to freeze half a dozen brass monkeys!'

Dover had got MacGregor so bemused that the sergeant was actually bringing the drinks over from the bar before he re-membered the point he had been trying to make. Ready to kick himself he handed Dover his large rum and peppermint (guaranteed to ward off chills on the stomach) and took the chair next to him.

'Good health!' said Dover cheerfully.

MacGregor let his pale ale grow flat untouched. 'Sir, this question of the Claret Tappers apparently knowing the exact time of your departure from the Yard . . . '

The beam of contentment faded from Dover's face. 'Oh, 'strewth, you're not still harping on that are you?'

'Sir,' – MacGregor looked round the empty pub and lowered his voice – 'the only way the kidnappers could have been ready and waiting for you as you left the Yard was if somebody inside tipped them off.'

Dover's mouth opened and then shut again. MacGregor was shocked to see how white the old fool had suddenly gone and, with the callousness of comparative youth, was inclined to attribute it to the too rapid consumption of the rum.

'Are you all right, sir?'

Dover swallowed. 'Somebody in the Yard tipped 'em off?' His voice was hoarse and rather unsteady.

'I can't see any other explanation, sir.'

Dover's blood ran cold. He wanted to make some jokey remark about having been nursing a viper in his bosom, but the words wouldn't come. In spite of all his whining and grumbling, the reality of his experience was only now beginning to come home to him. The Claret Tappers were for real – a bunch of ruthless criminals who'd been fully prepared to barter his life against a ridiculously large sum of money. They would, if he hadn't escaped their clutches by some miracle, have killed him. Dover shivered. But the worst was yet to come. He wasn't just any old, haphazardly chosen victim. On the contrary, he had been carefully selected. Somebody had set him up. Somebody inside Scotland Yard itself had actually planned and plotted to deliver him up to these merciless thugs. What a terrible realisation! 'Strewth, it got you right in the gut and . . .

Dover gulped down the remains of his rum and peppermint. 'Get us another!' he croaked and staggered to his feet.

MacGregor looked up at him in some surprise. That well-known podgy pasty face had gone quite green round the edges. 'Are you going somewhere, sir?'

'I'm going to the bog!' replied Dover with what dignity he could muster before making a run for it.

It was twenty minutes before he came waddling back.

'Feeling better, sir?'

Usually there was nothing that Dover liked better than a rosy little chat about his more intimate bodily functions, but at the moment he had more weighty matters on his mind. He went straight to the meat of the problem. 'Who is it?'

'I don't know, sir.'

'You're my Number One suspect, laddie!'

'Me, sir?' To his dismay MacGregor saw that Dover wasn't joking. 'But I wasn't even here, sir!'

Dover picked up his second rum and peppermint. 'And that's just where you were so clever, isn't it? You manufacture yourself a nice little alibi just when it's most needed. You weren't stupid enough to have me kidnapped while you were here, were you?'

There are some occasions when argument is a pure waste of breath and MacGregor could see that this was one of them. For his own peace of mind, though, he was anxious to get the needle of Dover's thought processes out of this particular groove. 'In the first place, sir,' he said, 'I wouldn't dream of being involved in anything so dreadful, as you very well know. And, in the second place, how could I possibly have known in advance that on that one particular night you would be working late and not leaving the Yard until eight o'clock? It's never happened before, sir, not in all the years I've known you. And, in the third place ... ' MacGregor hesitated. Surely he'd got a third place, hadn't he?

'And in the third place?' echoed Dover, looking roguish and waving his now empty glass suggestively.

MacGregor bowed to the inevitable. 'Rum and peppermint again, sir?'

The pub had been filling up and customers had begun to move away from the bar to sit at the tables. Seats were soon at a premium and Dover was several times obliged to repel intrud-

79

ers who thought they could come and sit at his table just because there were three empty places there. It didn't take much to put them off, of course. Usually one look *from* Dover and one look *at* him were more than enough. When they weren't, a growled 'bugger off!' speedily completed the operation.

'Sir,' – MacGregor came back with yet another rum and pep – 'why were you working late on Tuesday night?' This was very tactful because, like everybody else in Scotland Yard, MacGregor had heard the joke about oversleeping.

Except that it wasn't a joke.

It was the rum that must have made Dover careless as he was usually at pains to preserve his image. 'I dozed off!' he admitted with a boozy snigger. 'Mind you, I'd had one hell of a day and what with having to muck about till six o'clock just to spike old Brockhurst's guns ... Well, I just closed my eyes to rest 'em for a couple of minutes and it was bloody five to eight when I came to.'

'What time did you doze off, sir?'

'How do I know? What does it matter, anyhow?'

'Well, we've still got this business of an informer inside the Yard, sir, tipping the rest of the gang off. How could he even suspect that you were going to be so conveniently late that evening?'

'Second sight?' asked Dover, trying to be constructive.

'If you could just try and remember even approximately what time you dozed off, sir, it might help.'

Dover chose to take offence at MacGregor's wheedling tone. 'Well, I can't remember!' he snapped. 'So that's that, isn't it? All I know is that it must have been some time after the girl brought me the tea.'

MacGregor had to count up to fifty this time. 'What girl was that, sir?' he asked calmly, though his nerves were still jangling with the shock. 'This is the first time you've mentioned her.'

Dover shrugged off the reproach. 'Don't blame me, laddie! I'd have told you about her quick enough if you'd asked me. 'Strewth, there's nothing mysterious about her. She just came

80

into my room round about half past four, carrying a little tray with a cup of tea on it and some biscuits. She said the Assistant Commissioner had ordered it but then he'd gone out before she'd brought it. She said she didn't drink tea herself and, rather than let it go to waste, she'd popped in to see if I'd like it.'

'And you did, sir, of course.'

'Never look a gift horse in the mouth, laddie!'

'Then what happened, sir?'

'Nothing happened!' Dover was growing irritable under this merciless cross-examination. 'She pushed off and I drank the tea and ate the biscuits.'

'And fell into a deep sleep, sir?'

For once in his life MacGregor got Dover's full attention. 'Hell's teeth, d'you think it was doped?'

'Well, it's a possibility, isn't it, sir? I mean, didn't it strike you that the whole incident was a bit fishy?'

Dover scowled. 'Why should it?'

MacGregor stared deep into his glass of pale ale. 'The Assistant Commissioner's room is two floors below ours, sir.'

'So?'

It was at moments like this that MacGregor wondered why he'd ever volunteered for C.I.D. in the first place. 'It's rather unlikely, isn't it, sir, that this girl, whoever she is, would wander half way over New Scotland Yard just to get rid of an unwanted cup of tea?'

'And the biscuits,' Dover pointed out. 'I see what you mean, though.' A lesser man might have been tempted to attribute the girl's unusual behaviour to his own fatal charm, but Dover had few illusions on that score. He preferred to defend himself by attacking his sergeant. ' 'Course, any fool can see it was a bit peculiar *now,* seeing it with bloody hindsight. It's a different kettle of fish when you're on the spot trying to sort things out at the time.'

MacGregor couldn't see any future in pursuing that line of argument. 'You woke up about eight, sir? Did you leave the Yard immediately?'

'You can bet your bloody boots I did!' said Dover, astonished that even MacGregor was fool enough to ask such a question.

'Did you wake up on your own, sir, or did something rouse you?'

The spectacle of Dover trying to think was one to make strong men tremble. 'The telephone rang,' he said at long last. 'Yes that's right! The phone rang.'

MacGregor's head came up with a jerk. 'Did you answer it, sir?' Dover frequently refrained from picking up the receiver on the grounds that no communications could, with luck, mean no work.

'Of course I answered it!'

'And?'

Dover glared resentfully. Nag, nag, nag! 'There was nobody there.'

'I see.'

Dover resented MacGregor's quiet air of superiority. 'Well, what's funny about that?' he exploded. 'The phones are always going cock-eyed. It's the mice getting in the bloody switchboard.'

'Oh, it may mean nothing at all, sir,' agreed MacGregor soothingly, 'but it is just one more small point, isn't it?' He got his notebook out. 'Can you give me a description of the girl, sir?'

'Eh?'

MacGregor tried again. 'What did she look like, sir?'

'Somebody's sitting there!'

The lady who had been about to slide into the vacant seat next to Dover all but jumped out of her skin. 'Oh, oh, I do beg your pardon!' she gasped and, being rather sensitive, rushed off to the ladies' room to have hysterics.

Dover moodily watched her go. 'Youngish,' he said in answer to MacGregor's question. 'And hairy.'

'Hairy, sir?'

'She'd got a lot of hair, you fool! On her head. Sticking out!

82

Like they all wear it these days.'

'Could it have been a wig, sir?' asked MacGregor with sudden inspiration.

Dover groaned. 'How should I know?'

'Was she tall, sir?'

'Not really.'

'Fat?'

'Sort of average,' said Dover, conscious that he wasn't cutting too good a figure. 'She was just an ordinary girl.'

To tell the truth, MacGregor hadn't actually expected anything better. He really would have been a fool if he'd expected Dover to take any notice of a mere popsie when there was food and drink in the same room. 'Did she wear glasses, sir?'

Dover hadn't the faintest idea. 'No!'

'Was she wearing a skirt or trousers, sir?'

Dover grimaced with relief. 'I couldn't see, could I?' he asked. 'The edge of the desk hid her bottom half.'

MacGregor drew little matchstick men all over his notebook. 'She wasn't wearing a uniform, I take it, sir?' He glanced up to find Dover staring helplessly at him. 'She wasn't a policewoman?'

No, Dover was almost one hundred per cent sure that his lady visitor had not been a uniformed policewoman. 'Well, that's something, isn't it?' he demanded, infuriated by MacGregor's barely veiled exasperation. 'It must narrow the field down, for God's sake.'

MacGregor shook his head. 'Sir, there must be hundreds of women in Scotland Yard at any given moment. Legitimately there, I mean. If we're actually looking for somebody who slipped through the security checks – well, then I don't think we'll ever find her.'

'She was wearing a sort of overall!' crowed Dover, swelling with pride. 'A blue overall! Sort of shiny.'

'And as soon as she gets out of your room, sir, she takes it off and pops it in her handbag. In other words, we've no idea how she was dressed. If, on top of that, she was wearing a wig ...'

Dover caught MacGregor's pessimism and glumly finished off his drink. 'We'll have to have an identity parade,' he said.

Seven

What Dover had had in mind turned out to be rather imprac-
ticable. He'd had visions of lolling back at his ease while the
entire female work force of Scotland Yard paraded past his
totally unlickerish gaze. It fell to MacGregor to indicate a few
of the difficulties. The number of women concerned ran into
several hundreds and they would never all be available for
inspection at the same time. Then there was the quite unacceptable disruption such a procession would cause and,
finally . . .

'We'd have a strike on our hands, sir,' said MacGregor. 'Or a
riot. The Yard's full of Women's Libbers, you know, and they
wouldn't take kindly to being put through a process which
would strike some of them as being on a par with the selection
of candidates for the harem.'

Dover, looking more disconsolate than any frustrated pasha,
asked for alternative suggestions.

MacGregor was well used to doing Dover's thinking for him
and had come prepared to offer a solution. 'I thought we might
just stroll around, sir, and see if you could recognise anybody.'
It was a plan which relied rather heavily on the benevolence of
Lady Luck for its success and required a mite too much effort

on Dover's part to be entirely palatable, but the chief inspector raised no objection.

'Come on, then!' he said.

MacGregor blinked. 'Now, sir?' It was five past nine on a damp Monday morning and Dover usually required at least an hour to recuperate from the rigours of his journey into the centre of London.

But Dover had got his dander up. That he should have suffered the indignities of being kidnapped was bad enough, but that they should drug him into submission in his own bloody office was unforgivable. 'Now!' he repeated, and off they went.

By eleven o'clock, of course, all Dover's righteous anger had evaporated and his feet were playing him up something cruel. MacGregor spotted the danger signs and led the way to the nearest canteen. Dover sank down thankfully at one of the tables while MacGregor queued up for two cups of coffee and enough tasty snacks to feed a family of five for a week or, alternatively, to keep Dover going till lunch-time.

So far, the search for the elusive lady had been unsuccessful. Although he would have died rather than admit it, Dover's eyesight wasn't what it was and several women had already taken vociferous objection to the close and intimate scrutiny to which they had been exposed. At least two of the more delicately nurtured females were even now penning their indignant resignations and one stalwart trade unionist, who prided herself on knowing a rapist when she saw one, had convened a protest meeting of sister lady-cleaners for one o'clock.

'It's not been a very fruitful morning so far, has it, sir?' said MacGregor, sipping his coffee like a proper little gentleman and trying to shut out the sounds of Dover's uninhibited mastication.

'Knew it wouldn't be,' replied Dover through a mouthful of cheese and pickle sandwich. 'It was a damned stupid idea in the first place.'

MacGregor accepted the criticism with his customary

86

meekness. 'I think maybe we ought to try at night, sir.'

Dover's jaws missed a beat. 'You can stuff that for a lark!'

'It does make sense though, sir. You see, assuming that the girl is employed here in the Yard, she was obviously on late afternoon or evening duty, wasn't she? She came into your room about half-past four so she could have been on the normal day shift, but she must have been hanging around till eight to ring you on the phone and then tip off the gang. Now ...'

Dover reached for a cornish pasty. 'She could have rung me up from the north of Scotland,' he pointed out.

'I don't think that's really very likely, sir,' said MacGregor, dabbing at his lips with a real silk handkerchief. 'I was wondering if it would be a good idea for me to go along to Personnel and check through the time sheets and things. It must be possible to sort out the women who were supposed to be working here on Tuesday evening. I mean, if we could narrow it down to perhaps a couple of dozen, we could go and have a proper look at them. This way' – he dismissed two hours' hard slog with a wave of his hand – 'does seem a little pointless.'

'Now he tells me!' grunted Dover.

After this, the conversation lapsed and the two detectives sat on in the comparative silence of a busy cafeteria. Dover was mopping up the crumbs on his plate with a damp finger when MacGregor gave a chuckle.

'What's up with you?'

'I was just thinking about that young man in the typing pool, sir. Oh, dear! His face when you pointed your finger at him and yelled, "That's her!"'

Dover glanced at his sergeant without affection. 'He should have got his hair cut, shouldn't he? Puking little pansy! No wonder people are always mistaking these long-haired louts for girls.'

MacGregor had got a fit of the giggles. He took his silk handkerchief out again and mopped at his eyes. 'I thought he was going to have a fit, sir! I did, honestly. He went as white as a sheet. And he'd only popped into the typing pool to deliver a box of carbons!'

With cold calculation Dover proceeded to wipe the smile off MacGregor's silly face. 'My girl could have been a man,' he said. 'Now I come to think of it. In drag. Some of 'em can look very lifelike when they put their minds to it.'

The prospect of widening the field of search to include every living soul in the Yard was more than MacGregor could bear. 'You're not serious, sir?'

Dover's mind had grasshopped onto another topic. 'There can't be all that many women hanging about here after six in the evening,' he mused. 'Clerks and typists don't work that late and the men go on the switchboard, don't they?'

'True,' agreed MacGregor warily – well, you never knew with Dover. 'Of course, there'd be plenty of policewomen, in and out of uniform, knocking around still. And office cleaners too, probably. I'll check what time they come on.'

'Canteen staff.'

MacGregor stared at Dover in frank amazement. That was the most sensible remark the old buffer had made for years. 'Certainly canteen staff, sir! I wonder.' He looked around. Yes, it must be the hand of God! 'Can you hang on here for a couple of secs, sir, while I have a word with the manageress? It's a frightfully long shot, but ...'

Dover good-naturedly indicated his complete willingness to go on sitting at his little plastic table until the cows came home, though there was of course a price to be paid. 'Fetch us another cup of coffee and a doughnut first, laddie!' he leered.

The canteen was doing a roaring trade as the ravenous denizens of the law came rampaging in for their mid-morning break. The queue at the counter stretched further than the eye could see and the ladies whose duty and pleasure it was to replenish the dishes and dispense the tea were already beginning to glow with their efforts.

MacGregor hesitated. It was not, perhaps, the best moment for bearding the canteen's manageress but he didn't want to return to Dover empty handed. Screwing up his courage he

eventually managed to attract the attention of a harassed looking girl who was endeavouring to equalise supply and demand
in the sausage roll department.

'Mrs Fish, dear?' The harassed girl licked her fingers in a
distraught way before turning to unload another tray.

'If that's her name!' shouted MacGregor, trying to project
his personality through the intervening barrier of stolid young
policemen shuffling down the length of the counter.

The harassed girl pushed back a lock of greasy hair. 'In her
office, dear! Back of the cash register!'

Mrs Fish was not best pleased at being disturbed in the
middle of her own coffee break but she was the sort of woman
who would give a lot of leeway to a handsome face. 'Well, come
in then, lovie, and shut that door, for God's sake! Ooh' – she
shivered fastidiously and patted the corrugated waves of her
pink hair – 'it's worse than feeding time at the zoo!'

MacGregor accepted the seat to which Mrs Fish's heavily
bejewelled and scarlet-tipped hand wafted him and prepared
to explain the reason for his intrusion. He had barely got a
couple of words out when he was interrupted.

'Coffee, lovie?'

MacGregor shook his head. 'I've just had a cup, thank you.'

'Not that muck we serve out there?' Mrs Fish tut-tutted
briefly over such foolhardiness and raised her silver coffee pot
invitingly. 'I think you'll find this rests more easily on the
stomach, my dear.' The dark brown liquid streamed into the
bone china. 'Cream? Sugar? Chocky bickie?'

When the social niceties were out of the way, MacGregor
managed another half sentence before Mrs Fish chipped in
again.

'I *thought* you couldn't be here about the thieving!' she pro-
claimed triumphantly. 'I couldn't see even the ninnies who're
supposed to be running this mad-house being daft enough to
send a Murder Squad boy round just to look into a bit of lousy
thieving.'

'Thieving?' asked MacGregor, failing to make the mental

jumps necessary to follow Mrs Fish's conversational style.

'That bunch of light-fingered crooks out there, dear,' explained Mrs Fish with a contemptuous nod in the direction of the canteen. 'Cheese rolls up their sleeves and Madeira slabs stuffed in their pockets. They'd have whipped all the counter fittings out by now if they hadn't all been screwed down.'

MacGregor was bewildered. 'You don't mean the policemen?'

'I certainly do mean the policemen!' Mrs Fish was airing an old grievance. 'I challenged one of them only the other day. A mere lad, he was, hardly even begun shaving. "Don't tell me that bulge is your personal radio," I said, "because I know better!" Looked me straight in the eye, he did, lovie, and ...'

Mere politeness required MacGregor to listen to all the subsequent exchange of repartee, from which Mrs Fish naturally emerged as victor. A ready wit didn't, apparently, solve the canteen's financial problems.

'We're losing thousands a week,' said Mrs Fish placidly, paying more attention to the selection of her next chocolate biscuit than to her profit margins. 'I keep writing to that Commissioner chap of yours but for all the good it does, I might as well save my breath.' She flashed MacGregor a salacious smile. 'Still, let's not you and me waste our time talking about a mob of lousy coppers who'd nick the pennies off a dead man's eyes.'

MacGregor sensed that this was probably going to be his last chance of getting a word in edgeways. 'I wonder if you could give me a list of the canteen staff you had on duty last Tuesday evening. I'm particularly interested in girls who were on the premises from before five o'clock, say, until after eight. You are open then, aren't you?'

'We never close,' said Mrs Fish, getting what mileage she could out of that old joke. 'Is this about that kidnapping business, dear? Chief Inspector Rover, wasn't it?'

'Dover,' said MacGregor. 'We think he may have been fingered by someone inside the Yard. That's in the strictest confidence,' he added quickly.

'And you think it might be one of my canteen workers?'

MacGregor knew how sensitive people could be. 'That's only one of several possibilities,' he said tactfully. 'I shall be checking on the clerical staff and the telephonists and even the policewomen. Any young woman who was in the Yard on Tuesday evening is a possible suspect.'

Mrs Fish rummaged around in a capacious handbag until she found her massive gold powder compact and matching lipstick. 'Save your energy, lovie,' she advised, peering at her face in the mirror. 'It's Mary Jones you want. I knew' – she spoke rather indistinctly as she painted a careful crimson band round her mouth – 'that little bitch was a wrong 'un as soon as I laid eyes on her. Well, I ask you – volunteering for the late afternoon shift? No young girl in her right senses'd do that.' She paused and examined her maquillage before glancing across at MacGregor. 'That's from two to ten, you know. Ruins your whole evening.'

Taking care not to make a full-scale Palladium spectacular out of it, MacGregor got out his notebook and pencil. Strictly speaking he should at this point have broken off his tête-à-tête with the formidable Mrs Fish and gone to fetch Dover, but it was such a relief to be without the old fool that MacGregor simply hadn't the heart to do his duty. He squared his conscience by telling himself that Dover didn't like being bothered with details and he'd be just as happy snoozing out there in the canteen as he would being dragged into Mrs Fish's sanctum to listen to what might easily turn out to be a wild goose chase. MacGregor could always give him a simple and easily digested résumé afterwards if anything worthwhile emerged.

MacGregor gave Mrs Fish his full attention. 'You're basing your accusation on something a little more tangible than a willingness to work unsociable hours, I hope?'

Mrs Fish slowly raised eyelashes ponderous with mascara. She was an experienced woman of the world and had – God knows! – rubbed shoulders with enough members of the Metropolitan Police to be perfectly au fait with all their nasty little habits. Like putting words into your mouth. 'I was not aware,' she said cautiously, 'as how I had accused anybody of anything.' It was a sentence strewn with pitfalls for those with uncertain aspirates and Mrs Fish was relieved to have negotiated it safely.

MacGregor wasn't bothering about where anybody was sticking their aitches. He realised that he had antagonised Mrs Fish so he dropped his original approach like a hot brick. 'Tell me about Mary Jones,' he begged in a wheedling kind of voice.

'Not much to tell you, lovie,' was Mrs Fish's still coolish response. She sighed rather heavily and got up to cross the room to where a filing cabinet stood. She took her time about it and MacGregor was obliged to restrain his impatience.

'She's been working for me for just over a week,' Mrs Fish announced grudgingly, snatching off her diamanté-framed spectacles as soon as she'd finished reading. 'I interviewed her a week last Monday and she started work the next day.'

MacGregor frowned. 'That's a bit quick, isn't it? I mean, what about references? And don't these girls have some sort of security check?'

Mrs Fish glowered back. 'I can see you've never tried to run a police canteen, lovie!' she said tartly. 'Girls aren't lining up to wait hand and foot on you lot, you know. I have to get my staff where and when I can. When a likely looking counter-hand turns up, I can't afford to hang around for weeks waiting for all this blooming paperwork to be completed. You can't expect the girl to wait, either.'

'But the rules and regulations, Mrs Fish?'

Mrs Fish was sorely tempted to tell young Lochinvar where he could stuff his so-and-so rules and regulations, but she remembered in time that their conversation wasn't being conducted at that level of crudity. 'All the rules and regulations are being complied with, sergeant. More or less.'

'Oh?'

Mrs Fish automatically dropped her voice. 'I've got a little private arrangement with ever such a nice old chap in Person-

92

nel. I hire the girls, you see, and then we take up the references and do all the security checks afterwards. Do you follow me, dear? Well, when all the paperwork's finished and everything, all you have to do is put an earlier date on things, isn't it? That way everybody's happy.' She saw from the expression on MacGregor's face that he wasn't joining the general elation. 'I hope you're not going to start making trouble.'

MacGregor was something of a stickler for discipline but he decided to turn a blind eye to the peccadilloes of Mrs Fish and her nice old chap in Personnel, for the time being at least. 'Let's get back to Miss Mary Jones,' he said.

'Suits me,' sniffed Mrs Fish.

'She began work in the canteen a week last Tuesday, volunteering rather unusually for the evening shift. You were about to tell me what else was odd about her.'

'Well, she was never there when you wanted her,' grumbled Mrs Fish. 'That I do remember. Always popping off somewhere. I thought she'd got a boy-friend but I can see now that she was really casing the joint.'

'Yes,' said MacGregor, sparing a tear for the debasement of the English language. 'There were other things, one imagines, that aroused your suspicions?'

Mrs Fish's earrings sparkled as she shook her head. 'Not really, dear,' she said. 'I mean, the girl had obviously never been engaged in the catering trade before but, then, they all lie about previous experience. And she was a cut above the usual type of person we get here – socially, I mean. Most of my girls are – well – rather common, if you'll excuse the expression.' Mrs Fish's smile was patronising, if kindly. 'Of course, we do occasionally get a more superior type of girl, from a better home background, what's entering the catering trade at the bottom merely to gain the proper experience.' She cast her eyes down modestly. 'I myself began that way.'

MacGregor stared sullenly at Mrs Fish and closed his notebook. 'Well, we'll have a word with her, Mrs Fish. We can't afford to leave any stone unturned at this stage in our investigations. Meantime' – he nodded in the direction of the file which Mrs Fish had been consulting – 'perhaps you could let me have the names of any other of your assistants who were working in the canteen on Tuesday evening.'

'Mary Jones hasn't been into work since Wednesday,' said Mrs Fish. 'She rang me up mid-day on Thursday to say as how she was in bed with a bad cold.'

'She rang you up?'

'Oh, she tried to kid me it was the warden of this hostel place she was staying in, but I recognised her voice. They're always trying to pull that trick on me when they want a couple of days off.'

MacGregor opened his notebook. 'Have I got this straight? She was at work on Tuesday evening, the night Chief Inspector Dover was kidnapped, and on the next day, Wednesday. Then, on Thursday, she rang up to say that she wasn't coming in because she was ill.'

'That's right, my darling!' Mrs Fish sat back. 'And since then – neither hide nor hair of her.'

'She's cleared off all together?'

'Looks like it. It's all happened before, you know. Sometimes they write later asking for their cards and sometimes they don't.'

MacGregor chewed the end of his pencil. It sounded a bit thin but it was all he had got. 'Mary Jones lives in a hostel? Have you got the address?'

Mrs Fish reached for her file. 'She gave us the names and addresses of two character references,' she said. 'I expect they're as phoney as I don't know what, but you can have 'em if you want 'em.'

'Might as well,' said MacGregor with a sigh. 'And then I must be getting back to my boss.' He laughed awkwardly. 'He gets a mite tetchy if he's left alone too long.'

Mrs Fish didn't mingle any more than was absolutely necessary with the rest of New Scotland Yard, but even she knew all about Detective Chief Inspector Dover. She had gone off MacGregor during the course of their interview but she still had some vestige of affection left for him. She handed him the file. 'Here,' she said with warm hearted generosity, 'you can let me have it back later. It'll save you a bit of time now.'

Eight

'It's all go,' complained Dover, grabbing hold of MacGregor as the taxi took a corner on two wheels. 'Where the hell are we supposed to be off to now?'

MacGregor braced himself, both in order to counteract the next onslaught of centrifugal force and to overcome the sheer, mind-blowing irritation of having to tell Dover everything three times. Of course, he reminded himself in a sporting effort to take a balanced view, the old fool had been more than half asleep during the first recital. 'The Dame Letitia Egglestone Hostel for Single Girls in London, sir.'

'What is?' Dover was staring anxiously out of the window. 'Here, tell the driver to pull up at the next gents'. 'Strewth, those bloody curried eggs! I knew they'd do for me.'

'I did suggest that we shouldn't stay for lunch in the canteen, sir,' murmured MacGregor as he leaned forward to convey Dover's request to the driver.

'The trouble with you, laddie, is that you can't see further than the end of your nose!'

'Sir?'

'Where's the point in hurrying? If we cleared up my kidnapping tomorrow and got that bunch of murderous thugs under lock and key, we'd not get any thanks for it. All that'd happen is that old Brockhurst'd shove us straight off on another job up in the flipping Outer Hebrides or somewhere. No,' – Dover began to heave himself up as the taxi pulled into the kerb – 'better the devil you know is what I say. So let's not kill the goose that lays the golden eggs, eh? Softee, softee, catchee monkey! Get it? And open the door for me, can't you?'

MacGregor had a full five minutes in which to ruminate on these pearls of wisdom before Dover, looking much happier, clambered back into the cab and they continued their journey.

'What's the name of this waitress girl we're going to arrest?'

'Well, only question at this stage, sir,' said MacGregor, hoping to nip that conception in the bud. 'And she's called Mary Jones.'

Dover shuddered. 'Makes your blood run cold!'

'At least she's not Irish, sir!' laughed MacGregor. 'That should give you some comfort.'

Dover turned to stare at his sergeant. 'You gibbering idiot!' he snarled. 'There's *Welsh* Nationalists, isn't there?' He slumped back in his seat again. 'How old is she?'

'Twenty-two, sir, according to the form she filled in for Mrs Fish. Of course, all the information she gave may be false. Her referees, her place of birth, her age. Her name, too, if it comes to that.'

'And her address!'

MacGregor sighed unhappily. 'Well, yes, sir. I didn't want to phone and ask in case we somehow tipped her off that we were coming.'

'I hope you haven't dragged me out here on a wild goose chase,' said Dover with a certain grimness.

'How do you mean, sir?'

'This girl may be perfectly innocent and all she says she is.'

Nobody knew that better than MacGregor himself. 'She's just the best of a poor bunch, sir. I've gone through all the other women who are officially recorded as having been in the Yard on Tuesday evening, but none of them looks as suspicious as this Mary Jones does. Of course, sir, it would be a great help if only you could remember more precisely what she looked like.'

'I was drugged,' Dover reminded him indignantly.

'Not until *after* you'd drunk the tea, sir.'

If there was one thing Dover couldn't stand for it was a nit-picker and he was just about to tell MacGregor so when he realised that the taxi had stopped. He peered out of the window. ''Strewth,' he gasped, 'is this it?'

The Dame Letitia Egglestone Hostel for Single Girls in London looked more like Holloway Prison than Holloway did and its grim, granite façade alone had driven many an un-plucked rose into premature matrimony. When it came to the way in which the two establishments were run, however, there was little comparison as the insidious breath of penal reform had not yet penetrated the heavily bolted and barred portals of the Dame Letitia. Here a valiant rear-guard action was being fought against the permissive society with hard beds, cold baths, inedible food and carbolic soap. The staff of the hostel got little reward for their efforts, apart from the knowledge that they were doing exactly what Dame Letitia Egglestone herself would have wished.

Dover caught sight of MacGregor putting hand to pocket. 'Don't pay the taxi off, you fathead!' he bawled. 'Tell him to wait!' He glanced meaningfully at the hostel. 'We shan't be long. In fact, tell him if we're not out in twenty minutes to send for the bloody police!'

Miss Tootle, concealed behind the curtains of her office which overlooked the front door, heard Dover's little joke and failed bleakly to see the humour of it. Closing her book (*Witchcraft and The Black Art*) with a snap she crossed over to her desk and prepared to receive her visitors. She didn't hurry. It took a good five minutes for perfectly respectable women to penetrate as far as her office and men naturally had consider-ably more difficulty. Miss Tootle settled herself in her chair and listened to the rattle and clatter of bolts being drawn and chains slipped. Then came the murmur of voices and this went

on for a long time. Finally the slamming of the front door indicated that the callers had passed their entrance examination
and it was only a matter of seconds before Annie, the skivvy,
was tapping on the office door.

'It's the Old Bill,' said Annie, realistically miming a spit into
the nearest corner of the room as she stood back to let Dover
and MacGregor enter.

It was not Miss Tootle's first encounter with the police. No
one in charge of a hostel for single girls in London can avoid a
series of painful interviews with our boys in blue. Miss Tootle
had worked out a technique.

'Your warrant cards, please!'

Dover and MacGregor exchanged glances but complied
meekly enough with the order Miss Tootle had barked out at
them.

'Hm!' Miss Tootle tapped Dover's offering with her magnifying glass. 'This looks highly suspicious!'

'It's a temporary replacement card,' explained MacGregor,
getting in with a soft answer before an infuriated Dover re-
sorted to his fists. 'Chief Inspector Dover is an officer of considerable experience and seniority.' Dover's original warrant
card was still in the Yard's forensic laboratory being examined
for clues, but MacGregor didn't see why he should tell this old
battle-axe that.

Miss Tootle tossed the cards back across her desk and put
her magnifying glass away in a drawer. 'Make it quick,' she
advised.

Normally Dover left all the sweat and turmoil of an interview to MacGregor but, on this occasion he was clearly afraid
of having his sergeant eaten alive – and with that taxi ticking
away the pennies outside it was a risk he didn't care to
take. 'We're making enquiries about one of your girls,' he
began, half wishing that he'd listened more attentively to
MacGregor's briefing.

'At this particular moment in time I have eighty-four girls in
residence at the hostel. Which one do you mean?'

'Mary Jones!' said Dover to MacGregor's great astonishment. Considering the difficulty the old sieve-head had in remembering his own name at times . . .

Miss Tootle was consulting a small card index. 'Yes?'

'We shall want to have a word with her, of course, but maybe you could tell us something about her first.'

'What?'

Dover was beginning to go off Miss Tootle in a big way. 'Well, how long has she been staying here?'

Miss Tootle inclined her head and read the information off her card. 'She arrived just over a week ago.'

'Where from?'

'I've no idea. She gave me a home address in Birmingham.' Miss Tootle broke off to administer a stinging rebuke. 'Would you mind not scuffling about on the carpet with your feet like that, Dover? It takes all the goodness out of the pile.'

Dover's jaw dropped but, under Miss Tootle's steely gaze, he kept his feet in their filthy boots under control. 'Did the Jones girl give any references?'

Miss Tootle looked down her nose. 'I don't hold with references. I prefer to rely on my own judgement and the fact that all my inmates pay a fortnight's rent in advance and no credit. That usually weeds the sheep out from the goats.'

Dover was running out of steam. 'What about her friends?'

'What about them?' Miss Tootle didn't give an inch.

'Well, does she have any?'

'How should I know?'

'A boy-friend?' asked Dover hopefully. He looked hard at the chair standing in front of Miss Tootle's desk but the mental telepathy didn't work and he still wasn't invited to sit down.

'No men are allowed in the hostel,' said Miss Tootle with an air of such viciousness that MacGregor cringed back involuntarily.

Dover raised his bowler hat slightly and scratched the top of his head. 'Does she have any phone calls?'

'Not allowed, except in cases of dire emergency and through

me.'

'Er – do you know where she works?'

'In a café somewhere, I think,' said Miss Tootle indifferently. She put her card index away. 'In the evening, I believe. She's never in for supper.'

Abruptly Dover chucked in the sponge and it was left to MacGregor to carry on with the questioning. 'Is Miss Jones in the hostel now?'

'I should be very surprised if she were.'

'Oh?'

Miss Tootle shrugged her shoulders. 'She's skipped. Thursday, I think it was. Annie caught her leaving with a suitcase. She asked her where she thought she was going and the girl said she was just taking her washing round to the launderette. Naturally, we don't permit any washing to be done in the rooms or bathrooms here. Of course, the minute Annie reported the incident to me I suspected what had happened. I checked her room. She'd done a flit all right, but the sheets and blankets were still there and that's all I was worried about.'

MacGregor was getting quite excited and he even risked a glance of triumph at Dover. 'We'd like to see Miss Jones's room,' he said.

'You can't. There's already another girl in it. A Japanese. Besides, it wouldn't do you any good, even if our rules permitted it which they don't. The room was thoroughly cleaned out before re-letting and bears no traces of the Jones girl's occupancy. Annie has a very heavy hand with the duster.'

'You don't waste much time,' said MacGregor sourly.

'We have a very rapid turnover,' agreed Miss Tootle with evident satisfaction. 'Nobody stays here long.'

'No?' MacGregor refused to be down-hearted, though. 'Miss Jones's stay may have been short,' he said, 'but she was here for some time. Didn't she make friends with any of the other girls?'

'Miss Jones kept herself very much to herself.'

'Oh, come now!' MacGregor chided Miss Tootle in a rather

familiar way. 'She must have chummed up a bit with some-body.'

'There's Miss Montmorency, I suppose,' allowed Miss Tootle, if only to prove that nothing escaped her aquiline eye.

MacGregor rewarded this cooperation with his most dazz-ling smile. 'And where can we find Miss Montmorency?'

In for a penny, in for a pound. Miss Tootle consulted the man's pocket watch which she wore on a bootlace round her neck. 'She might still be in her room. She works in a super-market in the mornings and then goes to shorthand and typing classes in the evening. Or so she says. Personally I never be-lieve a word these girls say. Most of them are augmenting their incomes in some disgraceful way or another. If Miss Montmorency is in, you may interview her out in the hall.'

While she had been speaking Miss Tootle had pressed a bell on her desk. Now the door opened and the ubiquitous and omni-present Annie came shuffling into the room, bearing a tray which contained one – and one only – cup of tea.

'There was no call to go ringing that dratted bell,' muttered Annie. 'I was just bringing it.' She dumped the tray on the desk and jerked her head at the two detectives. 'Do they want any?'

'Yes!' cried Dover.

'If it isn't too much trouble,' said MacGregor.

'No!' said Miss Tootle, and it was her word that carried weight. 'I wasn't ringing for my tea, anyhow. I want you to go and see if Miss Montmorency is in her room. Fifty-three. Tell her a couple of policemen from Scotland Yard want to see her right away in the hall.'

'She'll have a fit if I tell her that!' protested Annie.

'Let her!' said Miss Tootle.

Miss Montmorency, however, was not in the least perturbed by the prospect of two flatties come to see her. She came bouncing down the stairs like a breath of fresh air and the American cavalry. She was a large, happy-natured girl who prided herself on having a really cracking sense of humour. 'Welcome to Colditz!' she called as soon as she was within loud-hailer distance. 'Have they told you you've got to share your Red Cross parcels?'

Dover was resting his seventeen and a quarter stone of flab and fat on a wilting umbrella stand. It was not the sort of thing he would have chosen to sit upon but it was the only piece of furniture in a hall chilly with shiny brown tiles and glossy bottle-green paint.

Miss Montmorency acknowledged the introductions with undiminished cheerfulness and listened eagerly as MacGregor gave a very circumspect explanation about the reasons for their visit.

'Mary Jones?' she repeated, wide-eyed with wonder. 'Golly!'

MacGregor was back in the driving seat again and relieved to find that Miss Montmorency was a girl who could give a straight answer to a fairly straight question.

'Well, yes,' she said, 'of course I *know* her. We've sat together once or twice at breakfast. Ugh!' She screwed her face up into an expression of disgust. 'The tinned *tomatoes* they give us! They're *simply* nauseating! *Much* worse than the porridge and that's saying something!'

MacGregor sketched a brief and insincere smile of sympathy. 'Can you remember what you talked about?'

Miss Montmorency launched into a series of callisthenics apparently meant to indicate acute shame. ''Fraid I didn't give her much chance to talk about *anything*.' She put one finger in her mouth and cast down her eyes. 'I'm a *terrible* chatterbox. Give me half an inch and I'll talk the hind legs off a *dozen* donkeys!'

Dover leaned forward to make his sole contribution to the proceedings. He gave MacGregor a sharp poke in the back. 'And don't say you haven't been warned, laddie!'

MacGregor pretended he hadn't heard. 'Did you talk about boy-friends, perhaps?'

Miss Montmorency assumed the mien of a Jersey heifer which had been crossed in love. 'Only *mine*, I'm afraid! Oh,

103

gosh, aren't I simply awful? I ought to go on a *training* course or take pills or *something*."

'What about work?' asked MacGregor, battling on with a brave smile. 'Surely you discussed your jobs. Did she tell you where she was employed, for example?'

'If she *did*, I wasn't listening,' moaned Miss Montmorency, who could have confessed to a dozen child murders with very little additional expenditure of emotion. 'I think she was a *waitress* or something somewhere – or did she serve behind the counter in one of those *posh* grocery shops up West? It was *one* or the *other*,' she concluded earnestly. 'Of that I'm *quite* sure.'

'Did she ever mention Scotland Yard?'

'No. I mean, why *should* she?' Miss Montmorency's smile was warm and only slightly condescending. 'She's hardly likely to confide in me if she's on the run from the cops, is she, sergeant?'

Out of the corner of his eye MacGregor spotted that Dover was beginning to exhibit all the classic signs of boredom. Time was running short. 'How about her family? Her background? Did Miss Jones ever mention where she came from?'

Miss Montmorency's ringlets bounced tragically from side to side. '*Frightfully* sorry!'

That was enough for Dover. He rose from his umbrella stand and rubbed his numbed behind with unwonted energy. Once he'd restored the circulation he began waddling off towards the front door. MacGregor grinned sheepishly at Miss Montmorency, thanked her hurriedly for her help and prepared to follow.

'She's got a coat she bought in Bath,' said Miss Montmorency suddenly.

'Bath?' MacGregor hesitated. 'Are you sure it wasn't Birmingham? According to our – er – information, she might come from Birmingham.'

Miss Montmorency smiled forgivingly. 'I do know the difference between Bath and Birmingham, sergeant! I'm not *that* potty. And it was *Bath*. She's got a blue suede jacket just

104

like mine, you see. With red and black fringes and big silver buttons. They cost the *earth,* of course, but they're really *gorgeous.* Well, one morning I was in the habitual *mad* rush and I *grabbed* her coat off the hooks outside the dining room. It was only when the label caught my eye that I realised it wasn't mine. I got mine in *London,* you see. From one of those groovy shops just *off* Bond Street. But Mary's came from Bath. The same shop – Naicewhere, it's called – but a different branch.' She looked anxiously from MacGregor to Dover. 'Do you understand?'

'Clear as mud,' said Dover, continuing his struggle with bolts and bars. 'Can't see what bloody help it is, though.'

'It does show that Mary Jones has been in Bath, sir.'

'Her and a couple of million other morons,' grunted Dover. 'And only provided her Aunt Nellie didn't buy it for her. Talk about clutching at bloody broken weeds!'

MacGregor felt obliged to emphasise the obvious. 'It's all we've got, sir.'

Dover believed that arguing gave you crow's feet and ulcers. He capitulated. 'Suit yourself,' he said. 'Borrow the girl's bloody jacket and let's get the hell out of here. This place gives me the creeps.'

'Not *my* jacket?' squealed an aghast Miss Montmorency. 'Oh, no, I *couldn't!'* The faces that confronted her were adamant. 'Oh, I *say!'* she wailed. 'Must you?'

Dover got the door open at last. 'Fetch it out to the taxi!' he ordered. 'We'll give you a receipt.'

'A *receipt!'* Whimpered Miss Montmorency.

'It'll only be for a few days,' whispered MacGregor, making a mental vow not to let Dover get his filthy paws on it. 'And we'll return it safely, I promise you.'

Miss Montmorency, overcome with distress, seemed rooted to the spot.

Dover broke the impasse with a bellow. 'Get a move on, girl!' he yelled. 'Chop, chop!'

The taxi driver, his eyes blinded by visions of early retirement after a few more jobs like this, actually climbed down and opened the door for his honoured customer. 'You've been a long time,' he observed gleefully.

'When I want your opinion,' Dover informed him, 'I'll bloody ask for it! And come on, MacGregor,' - he turned on his favourite whipping boy - 'get your cigarettes out! 'Strewth, anybody'd think they were made of gold the way you hang on to 'em.'

But Dover had hardly had time for more than a couple of drags when Miss Montmorency came over the horizon at a hand canter. Once Miss Montmorency got weaving, she wove quickly.

'I've put it in a plastic *bag*,' she said as she handed over her prize possession with more good-will than the two detectives had any right to expect. 'You *will* take good care of it, won't you? And let me have it back just as *soon* as you possibly can?'

MacGregor renewed his promise to guard the suede jacket with his life and handed over a receipt.

'I say,' said Miss Montmorency, 'I'm probably frightfully *thick* but I didn't quite get *why* you are so interested in Mary Jones.'

MacGregor smiled very nicely and, without being at all rude about it, began to close the taxi door. 'We just need her help in some enquiries we're making.'

Miss Montmorency continued to look a little puzzled but she pulled herself together as she saw that her prey was on the point of departing. After all, she'd spent a lot of time and gone to a lot of trouble for them. 'I say,' - she jammed herself between the closing door and the body of the taxi and waved a book of raffle tickets in the air - 'would you like to help an Indo-Chinese orphan?'

'No!' said Dover.

106

Nine

They got back to Scotland Yard at about half-past three, which left Dover with nice time for a cup of tea and a short nap before he had to leave to catch his train home. Commander Brockhurst had temporarily suspended his campaign to make Dover do a full day's work as even he recognised that there were limits beyond which you shouldn't hound a man who had so nearly sacrificed his all on the altar of expediency and public policy.

MacGregor hesitated. The old fool wasn't going to like this. He wasn't going to like it at all ...

Dover's eyes opened wide. 'What bloody house?' he demanded thickly.

'Well, hopefully, the one in which you were held prisoner by the Claret Tappers, sir.'

Dover blinked sullenly. 'Who says?'

'Well, nobody actually says so, sir,' admitted MacGregor, seeing only too well where this was leading. 'Nobody knows for sure yet. It's just that they do seem to have turned up a fairly likely prospect.'

'And I'm being expected to go and have a bloody squint at it?'

MacGregor inclined his head.

107

Dover settled back in his chair. In his younger days he had been in the habit of propping his feet up on his desk but with advancing age and obesity such gymnastics were now beyond him. 'Tomorrow,' he said through a yawn.

'We could be there in twenty minutes, sir,' said MacGregor. 'I've managed to get a police car from the pool and ...'

'Tomorrow,' repeated Dover. 'More haste, less speed.' He seemed to feel that this statement was a little inadequate. "Strewth, it's not going to run away, is it? Tell you what,' – he made the offer with all the magnanimity of a sovereign bestowing a knighthood – 'you pick me up at my place tomorrow morning. Ten o'clock or a bit later. Then we'll go straight to this house. Right? So tell 'em we'll have the police car tomorrow instead of today. Savvy?'

'I don't know if I can get a car tomorrow, sir,' MacGregor pointed out miserably, though Dover knew as much as he did about the difficulties in obtaining transport.

'All the more reason for shoving off now and trying!' snapped Dover. 'And take this with you!' He poked Miss Montmorency's blue suede coat. 'This is an office, not a bloody old clothes shop.'

MacGregor departed to make what apologies and pull what strings he could and at half-past ten the following morning he installed a somewhat subdued Chief Inspector Dover in the back of the police car.

'Know anything about women, sergeant?'

MacGregor was a bachelor – a shirking of responsibility that Dover usually found very hard to forgive. 'Not very much, I'm afraid, sir.'

Dover shook his head uncomprehendingly. 'You'd think she'd be glad to have me back!' he complained, but didn't enlarge upon the subject. Instead he stared morosely out of the window. 'Where are we going?'

'North London, sir.' MacGregor was armed with the exact address and even the map reference, but they were not required.

108

'Wake me when we get there,' said Dover.

'There' was a good residential area and MacGregor began to have his doubts as they drove through road after tree-lined road of well-kept houses. It didn't look at all like the kind of district in which a gang of sleazy kidnappers would have their lair.

'Flamborough Close you said, sarge?' The driver half-turned and raised his voice to cut through Dover's snores.

'That's right,' said MacGregor, leaning forward to peer through the windscreen. 'It should be a turning off this road. Ah, there it is! On the right!'

The police car swung sedately into a tree-lined cul-de-sac and made its way gently past one garden-surrounded house after another. The residences were, architecturally speaking, nothing much to write home about but they were all well cared for.

'Number Forty-six,' said MacGregor. '"Osborne". Ah, that'll be it! The one with all the cars in front.'

The nearer one got along the road towards 'Osborne', the more middle-class, middle-aged women seemed to be out, inspecting their front gardens. They were well wrapped up against the cold and the impartial observer might have wondered what on earth they were doing at such a horticulturally deprived season of the year.

'Osborne', admittedly, stuck out amongst the other houses like a sore thumb, but it must have had this distinction for some long time. Blistering paintwork, broken windows, gates hanging askew on their hinges, a herbaceous border run amuck – these blemishes don't occur overnight. The tattered posters stuck up in the windows were of a more recent date, though. Crudely lettered and obviously home-made jobs, they urged passers-by to house the homeless and join the revolutionary organization dedicated to providing Free Accommodation for All.

MacGregor, a detective of some years' standing, reached the conclusion that it was the cluster of uniformed policemen and official looking cars that had turned 'Osborne' from eye-sore to cynosure. He toyed with the idea of regaling Dover with this bon mot but, on more mature reflection, decided not to bother and gave the old fool a dig in the ribs instead.

Dover was barely given the time to shake the dust of the sandman out of his eyes before the door of the police car was torn open and Inspector Horton – all teeth, peaked cap and shiny silver buttons – clambered in. Dover shrank back in horror as the newcomer breezily introduced himself, insisted on shaking hands all round and then launched into an impassioned panegyric upon his own cleverness. Shorn of its grace-notes, this cleverness boiled down to the fact that one of his policewomen, handling a complaint about squatters and hooliganism, had noticed that mention was made of an old taxi. She had commented on this in an idle moment to the desk sergeant who happened to be reading an account of Dover's kidnapping in one of our more sensational daily journals. During the next few days these two apparently unconnected items had been kicked around for size in the police station until they had reached the ears of Inspector Horton himself. He had made the necessary connection and stormed, hot foot, round to Flamborough Close. Much emboldened by what he had seen at 'Osborne', he had checked with the Yard and was now unshakably convinced that he had found the place where Dover had been held in durance vile by the Claret Tappers.

'It all fits!' he concluded triumphantly. 'The uncarpeted stairs and hall! The continual pop music! The brown speckled tiles in the bog! And,' – he turned with a merry laugh to a stony-faced Dover – 'I shan't be charging you more than a double scotch in the Dog and Duck, sir, if I'm right!'

Dover pronounced his considered verdict on Inspector Horton as they all fought their way out of the back of the car. Finding himself at one stage with his mouth close to MacGregor's ear, Dover hissed virulently, 'Get rid of him!'

'Sir?'

'You heard, laddie!' Dover made the supreme effort and

110

staggered out on to the pavement. The gardening ladies of Flamborough Close rose expectantly on tip-toe and a coven of uniformed police constables, disciplined to the nth degree, stoically *didn't* exchange meaningful glances.

Inspector Horton, blissfully unaware of the black hatred he had aroused in Dover's ample bosom, proudly led the way, pointing out the sights as he went. Dover stumped along in his wake and MacGregor, as usual, brought up the rear.

They went up the garden path, through the front door and into the hall.

'Well, chief inspector?'

Dover hunched his shoulders. 'Might be.'

'I believe you were held in a room on the first floor, sir?' Inspector Horton mounted the stairs. The paint on the bannisters was scratched and chipped while the wall opposite was daubed with obscenities in red paint. 'Animals!' sniffed Inspector Horton before turning again to Dover. 'Any bells ringing yet, sir?'

'Not a bloody tinkle.'

'The chief inspector was blindfolded when he was brought in and out of the house,' MacGregor put in tactfully. 'Perhaps we'll have better luck upstairs.'

'Perhaps,' said Inspector Horton. He was beginning to feel rather anxious. He'd gone completely overboard on the theory that 'Osborne' was indeed the kidnappers' lair and had, on his own initiative, mounted a full-scale operation. Detectives had examined every square inch of the house and a team of forensic experts were still hard at it, collecting fingerprints, stains, dust, shreds of material, cigarette ash and anything else that took their fancy. Skilled personnel in the laboratory had been alerted and were already on standby and, probably, overtime. The expenditure of taxpayers' money and valuable police man-hours was already verging on the astronomic. A cold hand clutched at Inspector Horton's vitals! If he'd gone and got the wrong sodding house ... He pulled himself together and brought the full force of his personality to bear on Dover again.

111

'Er – the info from the Yard wasn't actually crystal clear, sir, as to which particular upstairs room you were imprisoned in. Of course I've got my lads going over them all with a fine tooth comb, but it would help if we knew which one we ought to be concentrating on.'

MacGregor gave Dover a heave up the last step. 'Wouldn't it be better, Inspector Horton,' he asked as tactfully as he could, 'if we concentrated on clues leading to the kidnappers and their presence in the house rather than Mr Dover's sojourn there?'

'Ah! Yes. Er – quite.' Inspector Horton was unaware that the detail about Dover being locked in the lavatory had been placed on the Secret List by the Commissioner of Metropolitan Police himself. That eminent personage had reasoned that there were enough silly jokes about coppers without providing free ammunition for more.

The emergence of a tall, thin man in civilian clothes from one of the bedrooms mercifully turned the conversation into less sensitive channels. 'Just the chappie I was looking for!' he exclaimed as Inspector Horton made the introductions. He peered closely at Dover's shoulders. 'Yes,' he repeated happily, 'just the chappie! Now, if you'll just let me take a sample we can settle this business once and for all.'

'A sample of what?' demanded Dover with understandable apprehension.

'Of your dandruff, my dear fellow!' said the tall, thin man, raising his predatory hands and revealing the scalpel and glass slide that he was carrying. 'I saw you from the window when you arrived,' he explained. 'Even from that distance I knew you were my man, eh?' He began to scrape some of the deposit off the shoulders of Dover's overcoat. The shocked silence which seemed to be greeting his remarks appeared to bother him. 'Well, it could have belonged to one of the kidnappers, couldn't it?'

'Just what I was about to say,' said Inspector Horton.

The tall, thin man was proudly showing his slide to MacGregor. 'Like guano, isn't it?' He produced another

112

glass slide from his pocket and clamped it firmly over the first before continuing. 'I found quite a rich deposit of scurf on the floor of the lavatory. You can practically wade ankle-deep through the stuff! What puzzles me, though, is that we didn't find it in any of the other rooms. After all,' – he chuckled deprecatingly, as he put his slides away in his pocket – 'the chief inspector can have spent only a comparatively small proportion of his time in the loo.'

'Maybe the Claret Tappers brushed out the other rooms,' said MacGregor, breaking into what promised to develop into an embarrassing silence. 'Er – what are you going to do now?'

The tall, thin man was happy to explain. 'I shall take this sample to the lab and compare it with those from the lavatory floor. If – as I strongly suspect – the specimens prove to have come from the same head, well, all your troubles will be over.'

'Thank God!' said Inspector Horton with a great sigh of relief.

'Personally,' – the tall, thin man began descending the stairs – 'I should jump the gun. There can't be two victims of chronic dandruff walking around in the same case.' He reached the bottom of the stairs and turned back for a brief moment. 'Pity it wasn't one of the kidnappers, come to think of it,' he called. 'I'd have liked to present the evidence connecting him with the crime in court. It might have made the Guinness Book of Records!'

Dover was not notably thin-skinned but even he had found this little scene faintly embarrassing. In a brooding silence he went through the motions of inspecting the top floor of the house, paying special, if unobtrusive, attention to the small, windowless toilet in which he had spent so many, not entirely unhappy hours. Finally he caught MacGregor's eye and nodded.

'You really recognise it, sir?' asked MacGregor, who knew of Dover's propensity for taking the easy way out. After all, if the idle old bastard claimed to recognise this house, he wouldn't have to drag around looking at others.

'It even smells the same,' grunted Dover. He had never mentioned anything about smells before, but MacGregor was pretty fed up himself and didn't pursue the matter.

But (albeit unwittingly) Dover had made Inspector Horton's day. That worthy man let out the breath he had been holding and thankfully uncrossed his fingers. His professional career and the future of no less than six little Hortons was now assured. But the inspector was not one for resting on his laurels. With a crash that all but scared the living daylights out of Dover, Inspector Horton leapt for the window at the top of the stairs, from where he snapped his fingers in an authoritative manner. Fifty yards away, in the roadway outside the house, a uniformed constable snapped to attention, saluted and marched smartly away.

Dover appealed to MacGregor. 'What the hell's he up to now?'

MacGregor shook his head. He found Inspector Horton almost as big a puzzle as Dover did.

Inspector Horton came bouncing back and explained the situation with an energy and enthusiasm that made Dover feel quite sick. 'The neighbours!'

'The neighbours?' asked MacGregor.

'All laid on, sergeant! Nothing for you big-wigs from Scotland Yard to do! They're all ready and standing by their beds, awaiting your convenience.'

'How many?' demanded Dover, cutting through to the nub of the matter as he so often did.

'Neighbours to interview?' Inspector Horton grinned happily. 'Three or four, that's all. I've had my chaps going round doing a preliminary screening. Knew you wouldn't want to be bothered with a lot of old fuddy-duddies who couldn't see St Paul's Cathedral at ten paces in bright sunlight.'

'Too true!' muttered Dover, the fingers of whose internal clock were already pointing to feeding time. He toyed with the idea of leaving the whole bloody business to Inspector Horton's chaps but, reluctantly, decided against it. Flamborough Close wasn't a thousand miles from Scotland Yard and senior Metropolitan police officers have ears like radio telescopes where dereliction of duty is concerned. 'Well, come on!' he said, seeing that Inspector Horton was just standing there. 'Wheel 'em in!'

'Actually,' said Inspector Horton with an awkward chuckle, 'I've fixed up for you to go and see them. It's only a step,' he added as he saw Dover's jowls quiver, 'and at least you'll be able to sit down. There's nothing in this house apart from a few old packing cases.'

Dover recognised the force of this logic. 'We might even get the odd cup of tea,' he observed as he made his way slowly and heavily down the stairs.

The first of Inspector Horton's hawk-eyed witnesses lived in the house directly opposite 'Osborne'. He was Major Gutty, aged ninety-five and the veteran of no less than three wars and thirty-odd years as a sales representative for a distillery. Confined nowadays to an armchair in the window of the front bedroom of his daughter's house he was, as Inspector Horton was anxious to point out, in a uniquely privileged position to observe what went on across the road.

'He's got all his marbles, too,' said Inspector Horton, staring down at the old man and speaking in a normally loud voice. 'He's just a touch hard of hearing, that's all.'

Dover snorted sceptically and, deciding it would be socially unacceptable to evict the old buffer from his comfortable armchair, sportingly settled himself in the next best thing. If either MacGregor or Inspector Horton realised that Dover had chosen the commode, they had enough sense not to say so.

Inspector Horton planted himself in front of Major Gutty and gave him the nod. The old fellow sparked instantly into life, reminding his visitors of an old gramophone jerking out its hollow and tinny sounds. Ever since one of Inspector Horton's chaps had called the previous day, Major Gutty had been rehearsing his evidence. He'd got it off pat now and only one

115

thing was going to stop him from delivering it. Luckily for Major Gutty's ambition to receive a congratulatory telegram from his sovereign, that didn't happen.

'The Bakers,' he squeaked, 'having lived at "Osborne", Flamborough Close, for three years, vacated the premises some eighteen months ago. The house was put up for sale but, due to the uncertainties of the property market and – I'm afraid – the over-optimistic ideas of the Bakers, a buyer has not yet been found. Until the last ten days or so, the house stood vacant and, apart from the very occasional potential purchaser, unattended. Then we began to notice that a number of unsavoury looking young men and women were hanging around the place, walking about in the garden and peering in through the windows.

'I told my daughter to telephone the police but, as usual, she chose to ignore my advice and had therefore only herself to blame when she and the other residents of Flamborough Close woke up one morning to find that a horde of squatters had moved in during the night and were in full possession of "Osborne". It was then of little avail to complain about the adverse effect such an invasion would have on neighbouring property values or to whine on about the incredible disturbances and annoyances to which we were soon subjected.' Old Major Gutty's watery eyes took on a malicious glint as he turned to the agreeable task of listing the disadvantages of having squatters for neighbours. 'Pop music and jazz blaring out all day long, and the nights made horrible by raucous singing and the twanging of guitars. The garden turned into a rubbish tip and old wrecks of cars littering the roadway outside. Inflammatory posters hung up in the windows.

'Certain foolhardy members of our little community here attempted to remonstrate with these invading anarchists. Their complaints were met with obscene gestures and verbal personal abuse. I shall not dwell on the manifold nuisances to which this gang of supposedly homeless people subjected us. Suffice it to say that one young lout spent most of his time

116

firing missiles from a catapult at such of our domestic pets as ventured to approach within range of his elastic. The young woman's behaviour was even more reprehensible. She appeared to be prancing round inside the house in a totally naked condition though, to be perfectly fair, the posters in the windows did to some extent block the view and made it difficult to ascertain the exact degree of her undress.' A thin dribble of saliva slid down the side of Major Gutty's chin and he seemed to be breathing more heavily. Still, he was a gentleman of the old school and soon regained sufficient control over his emotions to carry on with his story.

'One can but imagine the nameless orgies of sex and drugs that took place in "Osborne". Sometimes the house throbbed with noise. Sometimes it was ominously quiet.

'Efforts were made, of course, to contact the Bakers, but it appears that they are abroad somewhere and cannot be reached. The house agents, to whom they had entrusted their property, appeared to be quite helpless - not to say spineless - in the face of this rampant vandalism. They did send one callow pup - an office boy, no doubt - to appraise the situation but he was drenched with a bucket of what one hopes was water before he had even managed to ring the front door bell. He beat an ignominious retreat and was not followed by any successor.

'This disgraceful and scandalous affair lasted until Thursday of this week. Our children were terrorised, our men folk reviled and our womenfolk insulted. Petty crime in the neighbourhood increased a hundredfold and we all suffered as our bottles of milk and daily newspapers were regularly purloined. Representations were made to the police - without avail.'

'Ah!' Inspector Horton's deep voice fell as a pleasant change on the ears of Major Gutty's bemused listeners. He leant across and tapped the old chap on the knee. 'I did explain that!' he shouted, mouthing the words elaborately. 'You'd no *proof*, you see, that the squatters were responsible for the thefts. And, without proof, the police simply can't take any ...' He broke

117

off as he realised that the major wasn't getting the message. 'He's as deaf as a post,' he told Dover.

Dover paused in his examination of the contents of Major Gutty's medicine bottles. So far he hadn't found anything stronger than a rather pungent embrocation, but he lived in hope. Even a drop of surgical spirit would be better than nothing. 'He wants bloody shooting,' he growled, glaring balefully across the bedroom. 'Long-winded old git!'

Major Gutty was blessedly unaware of these unkind remarks. He recovered his breath and got his dentures settled again. 'Petitions were organised by some local residents and copies were sent to our member of parliament and the town councillor in whose ward we are situated. You will not be surprised to hear that we had no response to either appeal.'

'Can't somebody switch him off?' asked Dover.

'Then, suddenly, they were gone!' Major Gutty waved a bony hand in the air. 'Flamborough Close woke up on the morning of last Thursday to find that it had been miraculously delivered of its plague. They had done a moonlight flit. True, there had been a fair amount of disturbance and noise during the night – car doors banging and vehicles being driven about – but nothing more than usual. Still, ours not to reason why; eh? The occupation was over. The forces of evil had been withdrawn. There were to be no more smells, no more provocatively naked girls flaunting ...'

There was a welcome break as Major Gutty all but came apart at the seams as he was seized with a violent fit of coughing. Dover viewed the approaching disintegration with admirable calm, but Inspector Horton and MacGregor were made of milder steel.

'Christ!' said Inspector Horton anxiously. 'Do you think we should give him a thump in the back?'

'Good God, no! Do you want to kill him straight off?' MacGregor had once done a first-aid course and he tried to remember if a dark blue face was a danger sign. 'I think we'd better call his daughter.'

118

But Major Gutty had had a long lifetime of surviving crises and, before MacGregor could make a move to summon help, he coughed himself back into this Vale of Tears and resumed his seemingly endless narrative as though it had never been interrupted. 'A volunteer force of Flamborough Close residents was speedily organised to clear the worst of the rubbish out of the garden and the house was locked up again. Gradually our lives returned to normal. It was only then,' said Major Gutty rather nastily, 'that the constabulary finally appeared on the scene and informed us that the outrages which we had been trying for days to ignore were precisely the ones we should have been studying with the utmost care and attention. "Osborne" had not only been a den of thieves but the hideaway of kidnappers as well.'

This time the works really had run down and Major Gutty sank back in his chair with a faint puff of a sigh. After all, he'd just completed a performance that would have exhausted a younger man. Inspector Horton prepared to lead the procession on tip-toe out of the room, but Dover, popping another of the major's throat pastilles into his mouth, stopped him.

'Ask him how many squatters there were!' Dover saw the inspector's reluctance. 'Go on, man!' he urged impatiently. 'Wake the old beggar up and ask him so's we can get the hell out of this dump!'

It took the united efforts of Inspector Horton and MacGregor to rouse Major Gutty and, when they'd bawled Dover's question several times down his ear, they were rewarded by a glint of understanding in the old warrior's eye.

'How many?' he asked. 'I would estimate at least twenty, my dear sir. At least twenty. That's including the members of the' – he paused to lick dry lips – 'weaker sex, of course.'

Ten

'Clever?' asked Dover with an almighty sneer. 'What was clever about it, for God's sake?'

Inspector Horton wished he'd kept his opinions to himself and his mouth shut. 'Well, the kidnappers hiding their victim in a sort of hippie commune, sir, right in the middle of suburbia. I mean, who would ever have thought of looking for them there?'

'Not you, for sure,' said Dover.

'It was quite effective, though, sir,' said MacGregor who knew what Inspector Horton must be feeling. 'None of the neighbours would have noticed one additional body in that mob. And there'd be no extra bottles of milk or unusually large grocery orders to make people suspicious. On the other hand, sir,' – he saw from the scowl on Dover's face that a gesture of loyalty towards the old firm wouldn't come amiss – 'you're quite right. They were taking a considerable risk. Suppose the police had raided the place?'

Inspector Horton rang the front door bell again. 'That was very unlikely,' he said. 'Squatting's a civil matter. You know that there's precious little the police can do about it.'

'Drugs?'

120

'Well,' – Inspector Horton tried to see through the coloured glass in the door – 'we might have done 'em for drugs, I suppose. But you know what it's like these days. Large-scale pushing of the stuff and we'd drop on 'em like a ton of bricks, but a few kids smoking reefers . . . Well, we can't do everything, can we?' He rang the door bell for the third time. 'Damn the woman! I told her we'd be coming round about this time.'

Dover leaned up against the side of the porch. 'I hope you noticed how many of them there were in the gang. Twenty that old josser said, and he'd probably under-calculated.' Dover seemed rather pleased that the Claret Tappers were so numerous. 'And they had to dope me!' he pointed out proudly. 'I'm telling you – it took more than a couple of crummy villains to snatch me! There was some massive, high-powered organisation at the back of them, you can bet your boots on that! And now' – he returned to earth with a bump – 'am I going to be kept standing out here all bloody day?'

Just in time the front door opened to reveal young Mrs Youings standing there. The disagreeable expression on her patrician face was partly natural and partly the result of overhearing Dover's last remark. 'Frightfully sorry to have kept you waiting,' she drawled, making the apology as perfunctory as possible. 'I was just loading the kiln.'

'You're a potter, are you, madam?' asked MacGregor when the introductions had been made and the policemen were being allowed across the threshold.

'Only in a strictly amateur way,' said Mrs Youings who thought policemen should only speak when they were spoken to. 'Won't you go right through into the lounge?'

Dover was already there, and sitting down.

'Sherry?' asked Mrs Youings distantly.

Dover was the only one to accept – and that was solely because he saw no prospect of getting anything stronger.

Mrs Youings was not anxious to prolong the visit and got down to her evidence with admirable speed. She, too, had a good view of 'Osborne' from her windows and had observed

121

the squatters' occupation with a keen eye and mounting rage. She, too, had some hurtful comments to make about police inactivity and waited with scant courtesy while Inspector Horton trotted out his little speech. 'Yes, inspector, I know all about that!' she snapped. 'I happen to have an uncle who is a chief constable down in the West Country and I took the precaution of checking the legal position with him. While he agreed that mere squatting was not a legal offence, he did think that the local police might have found ways of encouraging the intruders to move on. However, that's all water under the bridge now. Is there anything else you want to know?'

Everybody waited while MacGregor, who was taking his usual copious notes, turned back the pages of his notebook. 'You're sure it was Tuesday evening that you saw these three squatters dragging a fourth man from the old taxi into the house?'

'I would hardly have said so otherwise, would I? As I told you, I thought the fourth man was drunk or under the influence of drugs or something. I didn't pay all that much notice because we had a dinner party that night and I was just drawing the curtains in the dining room. That's why I am absolutely certain as to the day and the time. It was about twenty-past eight.'

MacGregor thought for a minute. The time was about right if the kidnappers had driven straight from Scotland Yard to Flamborough Close. The traffic would be fairly light at that hour in the evening.

Dover's stomach rumbled loudly and, since he had managed to collect everybody's attention, he decided t put a quetion on his own behalf. 'That old fellow next door,' he said, 'reckoned there were some twenty squatters altogether. You, on the other hand ...'

'Four!' said young Mrs Youings, getting up to rearrange one of her hand-thrown pots on a small, highly polished table. 'Three youths and a girl. I don't think the girl ever stayed overnight, but I can't be sure about that, of course. She usually seemed to be around during the middle of the morning or the

122

early part of the afternoon.'

'But Major What's-his-name ...'

Mrs Youings pursed her lips. 'Kindly don't quote Major Gutty's senile maunderings to me! Just because he's as old as the hills it doesn't mean that he's automatically endowed with the wisdom of the ages. In fact, if you want my opinion, the sooner Major Gutty's put in a bottle and presented to the Royal College of Surgeons, the better!'

'The discrepancy is rather large, Mrs Youings,' said MacGregor. 'Between four and twenty, I mean.'

'They kept changing their clothes,' explained Mrs Youings impatiently. 'And they wore wigs. That's why unobservant people like old Gutty thought there were hundreds of them, but there weren't. I always,' she added with a patronising smile, 'watch people's feet. They are an unmistakable indication of character.'

After that, there didn't seem much point in the three policemen hanging around any longer and they took their leave. Mrs Youings hurried off to get her fresh-air spray and give the lounge a good squirting.

'Lunch!' said Dover when they were out on the pavement. 'Where's the nearest boozer?'

Inspector Horton's face fell. He scurried across to Dover's side. 'But we've got two more witnesses to see, sir,' he protested.

'They'll keep,' said Dover callously. 'In fact, if they're as bloody useless as the last two have been, it'll do no bloody harm if I never see 'em.'

'One's a child, sir,' said Inspector Horton, hoping to touch Dover's heart.

'You must be joking!'

'His parents have kept him away from school specially this morning because I said you'd be sure to want to see him. He lives right here, sir.' Inspector Horton was a quick learner and even MacGregor was impressed with the way he had learned to cope with Dover.

Dover stared gloomily at the garden gate which was being held invitingly open for him. Where you'd been offered one glass of sherry, he reasoned, you might be offered another. Graciously he allowed himself to be persuaded and waddled hopefully up yet another garden path. 'And God help you if this one's as big a bloody wash-out as those other two!' he growled, just in case Inspector Horton thought he had won himself an easy victory.

The Arnfields had been hovering behind their curtains and only paused momentarily for politeness sake before opening their front door.

'We saw you leaving Yvonne Youings's!' Mrs Arnfield twittered excitedly. 'I'm afraid we can't hope to compete with her beautiful interior decoration but, please, do come in! Gilbert, the sherry decanter, dear, if you please!'

The Arnfields provided a much better sherry than Mrs Youings did, but then they were so painfully unsure of their judgement that they daren't risk anything that wasn't the best. Mrs Arnfield settled coyly on a pouffe at Dover's feet and kept him well supplied with cheese footballs.

'It must be simply marvellous being a detective,' she cooed. 'I'm sure I'd never be clever enough!'

Dover beamed and then rather spoilt things by belching loudly. 'Dyspepsia,' he explained, thumping himself vigorously in the chest. He managed to convey the impression that this trifling indisposition was more or less on a par with a war wound.

Mrs Arnfield, her eyes moist with sympathy, passed the cheese footballs again. 'You ought to be taking it easy somewhere,' she said, 'after your ordeal. They must have no heart, those people up in Scotland Yard.'

MacGregor could have been sick on the spot. 'Could we see the boy?' he asked, breaking up what might have been a wonderful friendship between Dover and Mrs Arnfield. 'The chief inspector is working to a rather tight schedule.'

'Yes, of course!' Mr Arnfield glanced at his wife and, receiving her consent, trotted off to the kitchen where Arnfield Junior was being kept under wraps until it was time for him to make his big entrance.

'He's *so* excited!'

If he was, Master Arnfield was managing to conceal it quite brilliantly. A podgy seven-year-old, he was propelled gently into the room by his doting father. In his hand the bribe for good behaviour – a choc-ice – was already melting and he stood, lumpishly staring at Dover with hard shrewd eyes. Whether he recognised the awful warning with which he was being confronted, history does not record, but MacGregor found the resemblance quite uncanny. Indeed, if he hadn't known Dover's attitude to sex, he might even have been tempted to think that Mrs Arnfield ...

'Go on, Leofric!' urged the mini-monster's mother.

Leofric licked his choc-ice thoughtfully. 'I don't like that fat man,' he said.

Mrs Arnfield laughed uproariously. 'Don't they say some funny things, the little darlings!'

Dover placed a heavy hand on the conversation before it rollicked completely out of control. 'What's this miserable little bugger supposed to be doing here?' he demanded furiously.

Behind Dover's back, Inspector Horton made frantic signs to Mr Arnfield who responded with a pride which would have been unseemly in Leopold Mozart. 'Leofric collects car numbers!'

'Amongst other things!' corrected his wife, who had no intention of standing idly by while her son was sold short. 'There's his collection of foreign stamps and he must have got practically every picture that's ever been published of Bobby Buxton and ...'

'Suppose you just tell us about the car numbers,' suggested MacGregor, more sensitive to the danger signals coming from Dover than the others in the room. 'Young – er – Leofric has got a note of the number of the old taxi outside the squatters' house, has he?'

The Arnfields reacted to this blatant theft of their rightful thunder in their several ways but, as was usual in that ménage, only Master Leofric's frustration cut any ice. Bawling and screaming like a stuck pig, the child was shepherded out of the room by his mother while a sour-faced Mr Arnfield sourly revealed all to those heartless brutes who didn't seem to realise how impressionable some kiddies were.

Dover was as intent on cutting through Gordian knots as any latter-day and hungry Alexander the Great. He stared in disgust at the large, dog-eared exercise book which had been reverently placed in his lap. 'What the bloody hell's this?'

Being a nine-stone weakling, Mr Arnfield could only pray for a heavenly thunderbolt to fight his battles for him. 'It's Leofric's record of motor-car registration numbers,' he said stiffly.

'There are rather a lot, aren't there?' asked MacGregor, removing the compilation from Dover's nerveless fingers.

Mr Arnfield drew himself up. 'Leofric has been collecting car numbers since he was five.'

Dover turned wrathfully on Inspector Horton. 'What the blazes are we supposed to do with this load of old rubbish? Start checking the whole bloody shoot?'

'I'm sure that won't prove necessary, sir.' Inspector Horton took hold of the exercise book in his turn. 'The registration number of the kidnappers' taxi will naturally be amongst the more recent entries. I suggest that all we need do is start at the end and work backwards. It shouldn't be too much trouble to ...'

Mr Arnfield cleared his throat. 'Er – I'm afraid it won't be quite as simple as that, inspector. Well,' he bleated as three pairs of stony eyes were trained on him, 'you can hardly expect a little boy to be as methodical as all that.'

'Come on!' said Dover, starting to fight his way out of the clutches of the Arnfields' three-piece suite.

Mr Arnfield watched these struggles with an anxious gaze.

126

How was he ever going to face his son again if . . . 'Leofric does have a system, though,' he said quickly.

Dover sank thankfully back into the cut moquette and held out his empty sherry glass.

'Leofric keeps the numbers in separate sections,' explained Mr Arnfield, taking the stopper out of the decanter. 'One for the cars he spots on holiday. One for those noted at his grandmother's. Another for those he sees at school. And so on.'

'And one for those he sees at home?' asked MacGregor, getting hold of the exercise book again and riffling through the pages with more hope. He looked up. 'There are no headings!' he pointed out in a prosecuting counsel voice, having picked up one or two unpleasant habits in his long association with Dover. 'How are we supposed to tell which is which?'

'Leofric would know,' said Mr Arnfield, only too well aware that this wasn't going to be a popular observation. 'He might be persuaded to tell us which particular page is devoted to Flamborough Close.'

'Can't you pick out the page?' asked Inspector Horton. 'I mean, you must know the numbers of your neighbours' cars. Once you find the page they're on . . .'

But Mr Arnfield had to live with Leofric. 'I don't think that would be exactly cricket,' he said primly. 'We try to respect Leofric's rights as a person, you know.'

Luckily MacGregor was not the only one who had spotted that Dover and Leofric were kindred spirits. Dover had noticed it, too. 'How much does the little swine want?' he demanded bluntly.

Mr Arnfield went to find out.

Leofric wanted a quid.

Dover was indignant. 'The greedy little bastard! He's not getting a penny more than ten bob!' He turned to MacGregor. 'Give him a fifty-pence piece. I know that type. They can never resist the feel of hard cash.'

Out in the kitchen the seven-year-old succumbed to Dover's superior guile and agreed to point out the page containing the

127

Flamborough Close numbers in return for the shiny coin. He refused flatly, however, to return to the lounge.

'No skin off my nose!' grunted Dover as Mr Arnfield departed once more, furnished this time with Leofric's exercise book.

In less than a minute, he was back with his finger carefully inserted in what little Leofric claimed was the page they wanted. Whether he was right, nobody any longer either knew or cared. As Dover said, for fifty lousy pence it was worth the risk.

Dover's luncheon in the Bar Sinister of the FitzCrispin Arms was prolonged, predominantly liquid and very expensive. Inspector Horton, who found himself in – as they say – the chair, didn't usually patronise so recherché a hostelry but he had on reflection decided not to import Dover into the more friendly atmosphere of the Dog and Duck. Inspector Horton was well known and well liked in the Dog and Duck and he wanted to keep things that way.

At three o'clock the party, which not even the excessive consumption of alcohol had managed to make convivial, broke up and Dover headed back to the Yard with the firm intention of sleeping it off behind his desk until he could safely depart for hearth and home.

He had barely unscrewed his bowler hat from the grooves in his forehead when there came a tap at the door and a world weary man lugging a large, box-like container popped his head round the door.

'Dan, Dan, the Photofit man!' he announced as he squeezed himself into the room.

Dover could see his afternoon nap going for a Burton. Speedily manoeuvring his body he tried to deny ingress to the newcomer. 'Shove off!' he advised. 'We're busy! Come back tomorrow!'

Dan, Dan, the Photofit man was slim and supple. He shimmied past Dover and deposited his equipment on the chief inspector's desk. ''Fraid I'm under the command of a Higher Authority.'

Dover scowled. 'How high?'

'Would you believe the Home Secretary?'

'No!'

Dan, Dan, the Photofit man went on unpacking his goodies. He grinned cheerfully. 'How about Commander Brockhurst, then? Seems somebody sent him a report, which he read, about eyewitnesses.'

Dover was squeezing his way back to his chair but he spared a snarl for MacGregor en passant. 'You bloody idiot!'

Dan laid one of his Photofit pictures on the desk in front of Dover. 'Remind you of anyone?'

Dover nodded. 'The Queen Mum,' he said without hesitation.

'And this one?'

Dover groped for the name. 'That Goldilocks woman! You know, she was prime minister of somewhere.'

'Mrs Golda Meir,' said MacGregor, who would probably have shot himself if he'd had a memory as bad as Dover's.

Dan pulled out another picture. 'What about her?'

There was no holding Dover, now that he'd entered into the spirit of the thing. 'General de Gaulle!'

'And the last?'

Dover had been going to say Greta Garbo whatever the sketch looked like and he saw no reason for changing his mind.

Dan began to pick his pictures up. 'I should have stuck it out at the Slade,' he remarked to nobody in particular, 'and become a second Michelangelo.'

'What's up?' asked Dover and added, although he was not much of a one for giving his colleagues a pat on the back. 'I mean, you could see who they were meant to be.'

'They were meant to be your lady Claret Tapper - Mary Jones,' said Dan without rancour. 'As seen through the eyes of Mrs Fish and the most intelligent looking of her tea-ladies, together with Mesdemoiselles Tootle and Montmorency from Dame Letty's. 'I've wasted,' he added glumly, 'the best part of a day on that rubbish.'

'Well, you've got it all bloody wrong!' snorted Dover. 'None of 'em look a bit like her!'

'That's why,' said Dan, pulling his box of tricks closer, 'I've come to you, chief inspector. As I always say – there's nothing like a trained observer!'

MacGregor got out while the going was good. Dover, eager to play with his new toy, was quite happy for once to let him go.

It was an hour before the sergeant popped back to see how things were getting on. He found the office thick with tobacco smoke and Dover and Dan confronting each other across the desk like a couple of cock-robins engaged in a bitter boundary dispute. Photofit transparencies were scattered in irredeemable disarray round the room and both men seemed to be trying to gain possession of the same sheet.

'But that's *not* a Roman nose!' screamed Dan, whose earlier sang-froid had melted.

'It's what I call a Roman nose!' howled Dover. 'Why don't you concentrate on the bloody pimples? You've still not got 'em right.'

'Pimples?' wailed Dan, clutching his head in despair. 'You said *"dimples"* last time!'

'It's the same thing!' snapped Dover. 'Look, push off and let me get on with it in my own way!'

Dan laughed bitterly. 'Get on with it?' He picked up the torn and scattered result of their joint efforts and waved it in front of MacGregor's face. 'What do you think of that as the likeness of a girl in her early twenties, sergeant?'

'Well, it does look a bit like Henry Cooper,' said MacGregor. 'But, look, it's nearly time to knock off now. Why don't you give it a rest for today?'

Dan began to gather up the remnants of what had once been an efficient, well-regulated system. 'We could go on with it tomorrow, I suppose.'

'Er – no, not tomorrow,' said MacGregor apologetically. 'The chief inspector's got to go down to Bath.'

Dover paused in his efforts to fit Henry Cooper's face with a

130

new, and possibly Roman, nose. 'Says who?' he demanded indignantly.

'Commander Brockhurst's instructions, sir,' said MacGregor, conscious that the accusation Dover would undoubtedly make of sneaking was not entirely unjustified. 'He is most anxious that we should follow up that purchase of the blue suede coat. He thinks it's the most promising lead we've come up with so far, sir. He may well,' said MacGregor, gazing at the Photofit picture which now looked like Henry Cooper after drastic plastic surgery, 'be right.'

'Huh!' grunted Dover, ripping off an unsatisfactory hair line and hitting the nail on the head. 'All old Brockhurst wants is to get rid of me for a bit!'

Eleven

Dover saw the trip from London to Bath not so much as a railway journey but more as a prolonged nap.

'I hardly closed my eyes all night !' he whined as MacGregor removed a fistful of closely written sheets of paper from his brief case. 'It's my nerves,' he explained in a vain bid for sympathy. 'That kidnapping shot 'em all to pieces. My stomach's screwed up in knots and my bowels are . . .'

'Commander Brockhurst wants a full progress report when we get back this afternoon, sir,' said MacGregor, sorting the notes which he had sat up half the night writing. 'He's cracking the whip a bit at the moment. He wants these Claret Tappers under lock and key before they try snatching somebody who really matters.'

'Ho, ta very much !' snorted Dover. 'It's nice to be told you don't add up to a row of bloody pins, I must say ! Not but what I hadn't already got the message, laddie. 'Strewth, I'd like to know how many other coppers would have been left to their bloody fate like I was. I . . .'

MacGregor cut through the lamentations. 'I thought if we just started at the beginning and reviewed everything that had happened so far, we might come up with something, sir. A new line for further investigation might strike us or some piece of the jigsaw puzzle slip into place.'

Dover hoisted his feet up and rested them where some other unfortunate passenger was going to have to sit. 'Or pigs might fly,' he added helpfully.

'I thought that, if I gave a quick résumé of the whole affair, sir, you might correct me or . . .'

'Suit yourself,' said Dover, settling back and folding his arms.

Rather hurriedly MacGregor gave him a cigarette. With a bit of luck the sheer effort of puffing it would keep the old fool awake. 'The Claret Tappers seem to be quite a small gang, sir. We appear to be looking for a group of about four. Three youngish men and a girl. They planned your kidnapping very carefully. They infiltrated the girl into New Scotland Yard itself either to pick a victim for them or to keep tabs upon one who had already been selected. When they are ready to go into action, the girl gives you a doped cup of tea so that you stay on at the Yard until long past the usual end of your working day. This ensures that, when you do finally leave, things are pretty quiet in the street outside and . . .'

'That's why I went to sleep in the taxi !' crowed Dover.

'Sir ?'

'Don't you remember, numbskull ? When I said I'd gone to sleep on the taxi ride to wherever it was they took me, you came over all toffee-nosed and implied I should have been counting the miles or seeing which way the wind was blowing or some other bloody trick. Well, the reason I didn't was because I was doped. See ?'

MacGregor knew the futility of arguing and, besides, there was just the possibility that Dover had a modicum of justice on his side. 'My apologies, sir,' he said generously.

Dover was not to be outdone in your olde-worlde courtesy. 'And it was bloody coffee, you moron !'

There are limits beyond which even professional doormats will not go. 'Tea, sir! You told me tea ! Look,' – MacGregor

133

scrabbled through his sheets of paper and then grabbed for his notebook – 'I wrote up my notes almost immediately and you definately said . . .'

'Coffee !' When you get to Dover's age, weight and general lumpishness, you take your kicks where you can get them.

'It was tea, sir. Honestly.'

'Coffee !' insisted Dover, grinning like a sadistic jackass. 'I should know,' he pointed out, the incarnation of sweet reason and brute obstinacy.

It takes a couple of hours to go from London to Bath and MacGregor had visions of every last second of this time being taken up with a fruitless debate about non-alcoholic beverages. He swallowed his pride. 'Coffee, sir,' he agreed.

Dover sniggered fit to bust. 'On second thoughts,' he giggled, 'it was tea.'

It was probably only the fortuitous arrival of the ticket collector that saved Dover from some very common assault.

'We haven't,' said Dover when they were alone once more, 'found the girl and we haven't found the taxi.'

'No, sir,' agreed MacGregor. 'Miss Mary Jones, if that's her real name, is proving rather elusive and to date we haven't got very far with Master Arnfield's list of car numbers. Either that kid's nothing like as smart as his doting parents think he is or the Claret Tappers were using phoney number plates. Either way, it's my guess that they'll have dumped that old taxi by now. Run it off a cliff into the sea or burned it up on a patch of waste ground somewhere. Still,' – he sighed – 'we'll keep looking.'

'This case is full of bloody clues that don't lead anywhere,' grumbled Dover. 'Those two cons we slogged half-way across the country to see – fat bleeding lot of good they were !'

'Archie Gallagher and Lesley Whittacker,' said MacGregor, although he knew he could have called them Robin Hood and Maid Marian for all the difference it would have made to Dover.

'They'd never bloody well heard of the Claret Tappers.'

'Or of each other, come to that,' said MacGregor.

Dover, who wasn't quite as stupid as he looked, glanced sharply at his sergeant. 'Wadderyermean?' he demanded. 'We never asked 'em if they'd heard of each other.'

MacGregor was obliged to come clean. 'I checked by phone later, sir,' he confessed. 'I thought if there was some connection between Gallagher and Whittaker – other than the Claret Tappers, of course – it might open up an avenue that would be profitable to explore.'

Dover stared for a moment or two in silence. 'You know your trouble, don't you?' he asked sourly.

'No, sir.'

'You think too bloody much! Here,' – Dover's grasshopper mind flitted away to a more congenial topic – 'do we get lunch on this train?'

MacGregor prayed for strength. 'I'm afraid I don't know, sir.'

'There'll be a refreshment car.' Dover began to drag his feet off the seat.

'Sir, we really ought to go over the investigation so far. We're beginning to get bogged down. Every line of enquiry we try to pursue just seems to get us nowhere.'

'I couldn't have put it better myself!' agreed Dover, marshalling his strength before getting to his feet. 'Nothing seems to be any flaming good. Mary What's-her-name's disappeared into thin air and so's that perishing taxi. We've found the house I was held prisoner in and, for all the bloody good it's done us, we might as well not have bothered.'

'The Photofit pictures of Mary Jones might . . .'

Dover hauled himself up into the perpendicular. 'Stuff the Photofit pictures of Mary Jones!' he advised. 'They'll be no bloody help. I tell you – we've had it! The ransom note didn't lead us anywhere. Those two cons were a dead loss. And I'll tell you something else for free!' Dover had worked himself up into such a state that he'd even opened the door into the corridor for himself. 'This blooming blue coat we're going to ask about – that'll turn out to be a complete frost, too.'

MacGregor was so ill-advised as to try and look on the bright side. 'Faint heart never won fair lady, sir !' he quipped as he staggered along the swaying carriages in Dover's wake.

'Which explains why you're still a bloody bachelor !' snarled Dover.

MacGregor was still sulking when he pushed open the door of the Naicewhere Boutique in one of the more elegant streets of Bath. The way Dover kept equating the state of single-blessedness with a lack of virility never ceased to infuriate the handsome sergeant. He supposed that he ought to be able to laugh off all these slurs on his private life but, occasionally, he found that his sense of humour wasn't up to coping with the chief inspector's wit.

''Strewth !' exclaimed Dover, blundering into a rack of vaguely Oriental-looking draperies.

The boutique was small and dark and apparently crammed from floor to ceiling with weird and wispy garments piled in untidy heaps and draped over every available surface. MacGregor gave Dover a shove in the back and achieved the six inches necessary to enable him to close the door behind them.

Dover fought off a long woolly muffler which was threatening to engulf him. 'Funny smell,' he complained.

'It's new clothes, sir,' explained MacGregor. The buttons on his coat sleeve got caught up in some knitted garments and by the time he had freed himself he sensed that somebody was watching him. Peering round a pile of soft peaked caps in faded blue denim, he located the counter and, behind the counter, a pair of bright and beady eyes peeped up out of the darkness at him. The eyes belonged to a very small, bird-like woman who, once she realised she'd been spotted, moved forward slightly.

'Can I help you ?'

From behind MacGregor came a grunt of satisfaction. Dover, having found a chair, had duly sat down on it. In a better humour now that he'd got the weight off his feet, he took it upon himself to answer the tiny lady's query. 'Yes, I'm looking for a bright pink mini-skirt and young hopeful here'd like to see what you've got in gold lamé blouses.'

'We're from the police,' said MacGregor quickly, producing his warrant card and passing it across the counter. 'From Scotland Yard.'

'Are you here in an official capacity?' asked the tiny lady.

'Blimey!' objected Dover impatiently. 'We don't look like customers, do we?'

The tiny lady's eyes filled with tears. 'Oh, you'd be surprised at some of the people who come in here,' she whispered. 'They don't even pretend that they're looking for a wee present for a sweetheart or a wife. Sometimes I hardly know where to look. And such big, *hairy* men, too! Oh dear,' – she fetched up a sigh of incredible depth and pathos – 'when I think what this shop used to be in the old days! Such a nice class of lady! And such lovely wee clothes! People used to come from as far off as Swindon to purchase our all-wool spencers, you know, and our ...'

'Actually,' MacGregor broke in apologetically, 'we are making enquiries about this blue suede jacket.' He produced the garment from his brief case.

The tiny lady took it with regret. 'I know one ought to be prosecuted for selling such rubbish, but it's not really against the law, is it? Of course, in the old days before we were taken over – when we were still Clarissa Modes – we wouldn't have had trash like this in the shop then. Not even for the sales.'

'A girl bought that coat here,' said Dover, rushing in where poor devils like MacGregor hesitated to tread. 'Who was she?'

'Oh, I beg your pardon,' said the tiny lady, turning back the collar of the jacket, 'but this garment was bought in London, not here. You can see from the wee label. All garments offered for sale in this establishment bear our own label – Naicewhere, Bath. Mr Diamantopoulos calls it "personalising the merchandise".' The tone of voice in which the tiny lady made this last observation was probably actionable under the Race Relations Act.

Dover sat back and left it to MacGregor to sort that particular mess out.

The tiny lady's face cleared. 'Ah, I see! Not this actual garment but one similar to it.'

'With your label on it,' said MacGregor. 'Can you remember selling it?'

'I'm afraid not.'

'To a young woman?'

'All our customers are young. It's Mr Diamantopoulos's policy to aim at the teenage market.'

MacGregor tried the Photofit pictures and there was a moment of triumph as the tiny lady unhesitatingly picked one out. 'That's that poor girl they found butchered in the Crescent, isn't it? Why, it must be five years ago at least. Does this mean that you've caught the murderer at last?'

MacGregor collected up his pictures and got down to doing things the hard way. 'How many of these blue suede jackets did you sell?'

The tiny lady considered. 'Not more than half a dozen. It wasn't a popular line. Apart from being incredibly hideous and very badly made, they were rather on the expensive side for our clientele.'

'Do your customers have accounts?'

The tiny lady shook her head. 'Mr Diamantopoulos doesn't believe in extending credit. He's not very keen on cheques, either.'

'So most of your customers pay cash?' MacGregor's hopes dribbled away. It was obvious that he and Dover were marching resolutely up yet another blind alley.

'Sometimes it seems more like soap coupons and wee Green Shield stamps!' tittered the tiny lady, making a tiny joke.

Dover moved fractiously on his chair and, looking up at MacGregor, gave him the thumbs-down sign. MacGregor was loathe to admit defeat but there seemed little point in pro-

138

longing the agony. He risked one last question.

'Can you remember when it was you had these coats in stock? Was it recently?'

'Oh, no.' The little lady looked happier as she saw that her two visitors were preparing to leave. 'About a year ago. They were part of our spring stock.'

'And you'd sold them all by when?'

The tiny lady frowned. 'Two we didn't sell. They were returned to our central depot to make room for the summer stock coming in. That would be just after Easter.'

MacGregor immolated himself on a rack of plastic shower coats as Dover moved relentlessly towards the door. 'But that means you only sold four of these coats, doesn't it? Are you sure you can't remember any of the girls you sold them to?'

The tiny lady was genuinely sorry. 'I try to put everything that happens in here right out of my head,' she confessed. 'It's the only way to retain what wee bit of sanity one still possesses. And it may only have been three other jackets, actually. I can't recall if Mr Diamantopoulos allocated us five or six. We carry such a multiplicity of garments that it's really quite impossible ...'

Dover stood in the middle of the pavement outside and let the tourists flow round him. 'Did you notice how that silly cow in there kept calling everything "wee"?' he demanded crossly as MacGregor, having made the apologies and given the thanks, joined him.

'Not particularly, sir,' said MacGregor.

'Well, I bloody well did!' snapped Dover, looking up and down the street with some anxiety. 'Where do you reckon the nearest gents' toilet is?'

And it was on that note that the attempt to bring the kidnappers of Detective Chief Inspector Dover to book really came to an end. In the public lavatory at the bus station in Bath. Like most of the criminal investigations with which Dover was associated, it expired not with a bang but with a whimper and you'd have been hard put to it to find anybody who cared tuppence either way. The top brass at the Yard weren't pushing things. They'd decided that the kidnapping of Dover didn't herald a full-scale attack on the forces of law and order, and that was all they were really worried about. Even Sergeant MacGregor failed signally to work up much enthusiasm for the capture of the men who had taken Dover off his back for a few short, glorious hours.

And what about Dover himself? Well, our hero had been keen enough on vengeance at the beginning but it soon penetrated even his thick skull that you couldn't carry on a vendetta without involving yourself in a quite unacceptable amount of work. And work, in Dover's estimation, was the worst of all the four-letter, Anglo-Saxon words.

The Great British Public, of course, had packed it in weeks ahead of anybody else and would have responded now with a look of blank astonishment if anybody had asked them who either Dover or the Claret Tappers were.

Not that the Bath fiasco brought all activity to a grinding halt. Dover managed to maintain the appearance of being busy whenever anybody looked at him and kept MacGregor on the hop with various niggling little jobs. Reports continued to dribble in as police forces throughout the country and various departments in New Scotland Yard pursued their enquiries until they reached the blankest of blank walls. The fingerprint boys failed to identify any of the prints in the house in Flamborough Close. An old Austin taxi was found burnt out on the sands at Southport but whether it was the one in which Dover had been abducted no-one could say.

From time to time Dover made the odd telephone call, urging his colleagues to greater efforts but he knew as well as anybody that things couldn't go on like this much longer. Commander Brockhurst was wonderfully generous and it was only when he simply couldn't stand Dover making the whole of Scotland Yard look shabby and untidy any longer that he took the easy way out. There was a particularly dreary murder up in

Northumberland. The local police took one look at it, declared themselves baffled and called in the Yard. They got Dover. Within a matter of hours both he and MacGregor had disappeared into those Northern mists. New Scotland Yard smartened up overnight, Commander Brockhurst was seen to smile again and – well – who cares about a few disgruntled Northumbrians?

It was then that the Claret Tappers struck for the second time.

Twelve

For reasons which must remain secret for many years to come, Dover spent most of Maundy Thursday sitting in a tool shed on one of the better-known Northumbrian golf courses. For company he had a couple of oily grass-cutters, a rusty hand lawn-mower, and a platoon of spiders which kept peeping out at him from behind a mouldering heap of old rakes and brushes. By early afternoon he had consumed all the coffee and sandwiches he'd brought with him and was idly wondering if time would ever remove the marks which the empty beer crate he was using as a chair had cut into his ample posterior.

The shed was cold, damp and smelly.

Dover was fed up.

At four o'clock MacGregor arrived, soaked to the skin and looking worried.

'And about bloody time!' Dover welcomed him.

MacGregor sensibly refused to be drawn into an argument about the justice or otherwise of their system of watch-keeping. 'We've got to go back to London, sir.'

'Thank God!' said Dover piously and began to put some real effort into working the stiffness out of his joints. 'We'll never be able to pin it on that Sunday School teacher, not if we hang

142

around this dump till the bloody cows come home. I told Brockhurst that months ago.'

'We can catch a train at six, sir.'

'Tonight ?' Dover was understandably outraged. They'd been stuck up in Northumberland for three weeks doing damn all and nobody seemed to have missed them. 'What's all the sweat about ?'

'I don't know, sir,' admitted MacGregor. 'I just got a very curt message from the commander. They did want us to fly down but I pointed out that it would be much quicker by train.' MacGregor shivered. 'Especially in this weather.'

'I won't have time to pack,' complained Dover. 'And what about this murder ? Are we supposed just to chuck our hands in and leave it hanging in mid air ?'

'We've got to catch the six o'clock train, sir,' said Mac-Gregor patiently. 'That's all I know.'

'But, why ?' demanded Dover as they left the shed together and braved the howling gale and the driving rain outside. 'What do they want us in London for ?'

MacGregor had been feeding his ulcers with worries like that. 'They didn't say, sir. It all seems to be a bit hush-hush.'

Dover completed the manoeuvres which placed him on the lee side of his sergeant. ''Strewth, we're not going to be on the carpet for something, are we ?' He tried to search his memory but there were really too many sins of omission to keep track of. 'That's the trouble with people these days,' he muttered obscurely.

It was difficult talking in those near hurricane conditions but MacGregor made the effort. 'What is, sir ?'

'Always writing to their bloody M P s !' shouted Dover, clutching at his bowler hat. 'Do no more than rest your hand in a friendly way on their bleeding shoulder and they're bloody threatening you with assault.' However, Dover was never one to waste his time on theoretical calamities when there were more pressing problems close at hand. 'How much further to this bloody car ?'

'It's just by the ninth tee, sir !' screamed MacGregor, the wind tearing the words out of his throat. 'Only half a mile !'

'Jesus !' gasped Dover and, not being inhibited by any false pride, grabbed hold of MacGregor's arm and generously allowed him to share the burden.

British Rail was up to its usual tricks and so it was two o'clock in the morning before Dover and MacGregor clambered wearily up the steps of New Scotland Yard and passed through its portals. Even at that ungodly hour there was an air of suppressed excitement about the place which MacGregor found reassuring. Nothing that Dover did or didn't do could have got things buzzing like that.

Commander Brockhurst was waiting for them in his office. He was stripped down to his shirt sleeves and silk braces and was, figuratively speaking, wearing his naval hat. This was the term disrespectful subordinates used for the occasions when the commander saw himself, blue of eye, tanned of skin and firm of jaw, standing foresquare on the bridge and running a tight ship. It was a bit of play-acting that usually presaged squalls ahead.

Dover and MacGregor were, most untypically, invited to sit down while Commander Brockhurst completed the nautical scene by lighting a rather nasty-looking pipe.

'What I have to tell you,' he began, making smoke in a way that would have warmed the heart of any destroyer captain, 'is strictly confidential. You're not to breathe a word of it to anybody inside this building, never mind outside it.' He caught sight of the silly smirk on MacGregor's face and hastened to make the correction. 'Except for the other members of the special squad which is being put together for this operation. Now, is the need for absolute secrecy understood ?'

'Yes, sir !'

'You, too, Dover ?'

Dover endeavoured to terminate his jaw-cracking yawn prematurely with the usual disastrous results. Seething with impatience Commander Brockhurst took the watering eyes and contorted features of his *bête noire* as indicating assent

'The Claret Tappers have pulled off another kidnapping job !'

If Commander Brockhurst had expected to startle Dover and MacGregor out of their skins with the news, he was disappointed. They had already worked out for themselves that another kidnapping was a possible explanation for their abrupt recall to London.

'A police officer again, sir ?' asked MacGregor.

'The three-month-old grandson of the Prime Minister !'

This time the reaction was all that Commander Brockhurst could have wished. MacGregor's jaw dropped with a click that was all but audible and even Dover produced a strangled ''strewth', from a dry throat.

'I'll bet that's put the cat amongst the pigeons,' said MacGregor shakily. 'Gosh !'

'I hope you appreciate the heavy responsibility this places on your shoulders, Dover !'

Dover stared pop-eyed across the desk at the commander and swallowed painfully. His bemused brain managed to re-collect that some have greatness thrust upon them – but this was ridiculous. 'You're putting me in charge, sir ?' he asked.

Commander Brockhurst caught his pipe just in time and cursed mightily as some of the hot ashes spilled out onto his hand. His reply to Dover's timid query was appropriately salty but, shortened and expurgated of all obscenities, it still amounted to 'no'. 'The Commissioner, himself, is in overall control, of course, but I'm the one who'll be doing the real work. They're all trying to get in on the act,' added Commander Brockhurst bitterly. 'Special Branch, the Ministry of Defence, the Regional Crime Squad from where the kid was snatched . . . Good God, I've even had an inspector from Motorways Patrol on the blower this evening trying to stick his twopennyworth in. And that's not mentioning that bloody MP who reckons he ought to be running the show because his younger brother once thought of becoming a police cadet.'

145

MacGregor looked up. 'So the kidnapping's not entirely secret, sir?'

'Well,' – Commander Brockhurst had the grace to look a little sheepish – 'there has been some slight leakage, of course, but it's not got to go any further. We don't want the general public getting hold of the story.'

Meanwhile Dover had been experiencing a faint twinge of sympathy for Commander Brockhurst. It was a lousy business when you got yourself lumbered with a job that was destined to involve you in endless labour and then end in tears. Fortified by a lifetime's experience of shirking, Dover had spotted a way out and now generously offered it to his superior. 'You want to tell 'em where to stick it!' he advised. 'Kidnapping's not your pigeon. You're the boss of the Murder Squad and kidnapping's not murder, is it?'

Commander Brockhurst had neither the time nor the inclination to ponder on the mystery of how Dover always alighted with such unerring accuracy on the inessentials of any problem. 'I have been put in charge of this investigation, Dover, for two damned good reasons. One – it *is* a murder case. The Claret Tappers killed the au pair girl who'd been left in charge of the baby. And, two – you're the only person who's been in direct contact with the kidnapping gang and you happen to be under my command. Now, let's get one thing straight right at the beginning, Dover!' Commander Brockhurst leaned across his desk and thrust his chin out more pugnaciously than ever. 'Whatever else happens, I intend to emerge from this business smelling of roses. If, to achieve this, I have to wash my hands in your blood, that's perfectly OK by me. Get it?'

Dover got it all right and sank back miserably in his chair, his pasty face growing gradually pastier as he contemplated the awful prospect that lay ahead of him. 'Strewth, he'd be lucky if he sneaked more than a couple of days off for the next bloody fortnight!

Meanwhile MacGregor was looking all bright-eyed and eager. 'How do we know that this kidnapping is the work of the

146

Claret Tappers, sir ? Have they already made contact ?'

'They have,' said Commander Brockhurst grimly. He was really no fonder of clever young sergeants than he was of addle-pated old chief inspectors.

'It might just be another gang using the Claret Tappers' name, sir, in order to put us off the scent. After all, the Claret Tappers did get a tremendous amount of publicity when Chief Inspector Dover was . . .'

'Sergeant !' Commander Brockhurst remembered what they'd taught him on that man-management course and modified his tone to the merely brusque. 'In the message that we got from the gang who've kidnapped the Prime Minister's grandchild, mention was made of the exact room in which Mr Dover here was detained in that house in Flamborough Close. Now, nobody knew about that except a tiny handful of people here at the Yard and the kidnappers themselves. Right ?'

'Well,' began MacGregor.

Commander Brockhurst rolled right over him. 'Suppose you keep your questions until you're in possession of all the facts, sergeant.'

'I'm sorry, sir.'

Commander Brockhurst cleared his throat and Dover realised with a sinking heart that they were in for a long night. He regretted not having made a brief stop-off earlier but he had thought it wiser not to keep the commander waiting. Should he excuse himself now, or try and think about something else in the hope that it would pass off ?

'Dover ! Are you listening, man ?'

Dover blinked. Loud-mouthed bully ! 'I'm all ears,' he grunted.

'Well, I hope so, because if there's a cock-up this time, I will personally dismember you with a blunt knife ! Now, I'm going to give you a brief outline of what's happened so far, just to put you in the picture.'

'May we ask questions, sir ?' MacGregor's face was the picture of innocence.

147

Commander Brockhurst would have liked to say 'no' but knew he couldn't. 'So long as you keep 'em short and to the point,' he conceded grudgingly. 'Now then, as far as we are aware at the moment, the kidnapping took place sometime yesterday morning. Round about ten o'clock is the guess, but we could be out an hour or more either way. The Sleights live in a pretty isolated house on the outskirts of the village and there were, to the best of our knowledge, no witnesses to the kidnapping.' Although he wasn't really used to dealing with Dover, Commander Brockhurst seemed to know by instinct that you had to spell it all out slowly for the old fool. 'The Sleights are the parents of the missing child. And Mrs Sleight, let me remind you once again, is the Prime Minister's youngest daughter.'

'I remember her wedding,' said MacGregor fatuously.

'Wednesday,' Commander Brockhurst went on, making a mental note to delay MacGregor's next promotion, if any, by at least a year, 'is Mrs Sleight's hospital day. By that I mean she goes off to the nearby town of Granbury to dish out library books in the local hospital or engage in other such charitable work. While she is away, the child – Rodney Colin Murdoch, would you believe? – is left in the care of the au pair girl. Mr Sleight is a solicitor and he has an office in Granbury. Naturally, he wasn't at home yesterday morning, either. There are no other servants and nobody else lives in the house. No tradesmen call on a Wednesday and the milk and morning post and the newspapers all come before eight o'clock.'

MacGregor raised a hand. Dover would have liked to raise one, too, but for a different reason. 'Was the fact that the au pair girl was alone with the baby on Wednesday generally known, sir?'

'People in the area would know for sure, sergeant. There's a lot of interest taken in the Sleights's doings, with her being related to the PM. Strangers could have found out easily enough, I reckon. Naturally I'm having enquiries made in case anybody's been over-inquisitive lately.'

'The au pair girl could have been the source of the kidnappers' information, sir.'

Give 'em an inch, thought the commander bitterly. 'That thought had crossed my mind, thank you, sergeant,' he said sarcastically. 'Now, to return to the actual kidnapping. We think the kidnappers drove up to the house at about ten o'clock. The baby would have been outside in its pram because the weather down there was cold but fine. At some stage during the kidnapping, the au pair girl was shot and killed outright. Her name was Greta van Pronk, incidentally. Age eighteen. Dutch. Been over here with the Sleights for about six months. We don't know why she was killed. She could have been trying to stop the kidnappers or they were afraid she would be able to identify them or raise the alarm too soon or anything.'

'She might have known who they were, sir,' said the unsinkable MacGregor. 'Suppose she'd given them the information? She might not have realised what was involved and, naturally, they couldn't trust her to keep her mouth shut.'

'I'm well aware of all those possibilities, thank you, sergeant!' Commander Brockhurst began to wonder if he hadn't been a bit hard on Dover all these years. With a clever young devil like MacGregor tied round your neck twenty-four hours a day ... 'We're following up every line of enquiry, though Mrs Sleight claims the girl was very quiet and didn't go out much at all. She had a boy friend back in Holland. Now then, where was I?' Commander Brockhurst caught MacGregor's eye and dared him to provide the answer. 'Ah, did I mention that the kidnappers used an old Post Office van for the job? That'll be virtually untraceable if they did. Those little red vans are always buzzing about and nobody gives 'em a second glance.'

'Stolen, sir?'

'Not as far as we know. They're easy enough to get hold of, government surplus. All you'd need is a transfer to stick the royal cipher on the side and you're away. Or paint it on,' he added glumly.

'No windows,' Dover pointed out, on the grounds that every little helps.

'Quite,' said Commander Brockhurst.

MacGregor still had to play it clever, of course. 'It's an interesting repetition of the *modus operandi,* though, isn't it, sir?'

'Is it?'

MacGregor smiled patronisingly at the commander. Of course, he wasn't anything like as thick as Dover but... 'Their use of discarded public utility vehicles, sir, so as to avoid calling attention to themselves. First a London taxi in London and then a little red Post Office van in the country. What could be more inconspicuous?'

'And you couldn't look in and see it was a baby and not letters,' said Dover, just to show he was still there, 'because there wouldn't be any bloody windows.'

'We'd better get on,' said Commander Brockhurst wearily. 'The au pair girl's body was dragged out of sight into the shrubbery and the empty pram was hidden there, too. At about four o'clock Mrs Sleight came home – she has her own car. She thought at first that Greta had got the baby out for a walk although it was beginning to grow dark. Then she found the washing-up half-done in the kitchen, no signs of anybody having had lunch and the baby's feed still in the fridge. Once her suspicions were aroused she soon found Greta's body and the empty pram. She phoned her father in Downing Street immediately and that's when things began to hum.'

'I'll bet!' chuckled Dover.

'We're doing no more than we'd do in any case of kidnapping,' said Commander Brockhurst self-righteously, until he remembered to whom he was speaking. 'Of juvenile kidnapping,' he amended lamely. 'Er, yes – well, actually we'd already received a message at the Yard before the PM's people got on to us, but nobody'd had time to do much about it. The first reaction was that it was a hoax, of course. Somebody – a man, no distinguishing accent – rang up the Church Times and told

the girl on the switchboard there to take a message. He didn't
give her time to write it down properly but she got the gist of it
all right. The Claret Tappers had kidnapped the grandson of
the Prime Minister and he would eventually be returned unharmed provided all their demands were met. He - the caller,
that is - pointed out that no harm had come to Chief Inspector
Dover when he was in their hands but that, equally, they hadn't
hesitated to kill the au pair girl when she got in their way. He
offered this as evidence that the gang could be perfectly
reasonable or perfectly ruthless, according to how they were
treated.'

'That's meant to reassure people that the baby will be quite
safe if the ransom's paid,' said MacGregor wisely. 'That's
always the danger in kidnapping cases. A dead victim's a
damned sight less dangerous and less trouble than a live one.
Did they offer any proof that they actually had the Sleight
baby, sir ?'

'They described what the kid was wearing,' said Commander Brockhurst. 'It seemed to fit.'

'And they actually mentioned that they'd kept Mr Dover
locked in the lavatory, did they, sir ?'

The scowl that Commander Brockhurst produced wouldn't
have looked out of place on Dover's ugly mug. 'I've already
said that, sergeant ! Don't keep harping on it !'

'Sorry, sir,' murmured MacGregor, knowing that he had to
keep on the right side of the commander if ever he was to secure
his release from Dover. 'Is there anything else ?'

Commander Brockhurst began to relight his pipe. 'Only that
we were warned to start collecting half a million pounds in
fivers and tenners and to await further instructions. There's
also some rubbish about the release of prisoners but there are
no details as yet.'

There was a pause with everybody in the room thinking and
nobody saying anything. Dover was having quite a job keeping
his eyes open, but being dead scared of Commander
Brockhurst helped. MacGregor had been taking notes and

151

now, as he frowned in deep thought, he began to tap his teeth with his pencil. The noise was just beginning to grate on everybody's nerves when MacGregor broke off to ask yet another question.

'Why did the kidnappers ring the Church Times, sir ?'

Dover leapt on what bit of a bandwaggon presented itself. 'I was wondering about that.'

Commander Brockhurst looked highly sceptical but it was getting late and there was little kudos to be gained from cutting Dover down to size. 'We're not sure why they picked on the Church Times,' he admitted. 'My own personal theory is that there were a number of reasons. In the first place, it's a responsible journal staffed by responsible people. This would ensure that the Claret Tappers' message was passed on. Secondly, it's highly unlikely that the message would be recorded. You know what national newspaper offices are like these days. Tape-recorders all over the blooming place. Same with the Yard, of course. Anybody on our switchboard would have tried to record that message the minute he suspected what it was.'

'That seems a very likely explanation, sir,' said MacGregor with the smile of a hopeful sycophant.

'I'm glad it meets with your approval, sergeant !' Commander Brockhurst laid his pipe aside because it was really making him feel quite sick. 'Well, that's put you both in the picture ! Now, we're tackling this problem from every conceivable angle, but that's not your concern. What I want you two to do is to go over every single detail of Chief Inspector Dover's kidnapping. Everything, you understand ! I want the whole thing re-analysed from top to toe. Got it ? Re-examine every fact in the light of this latest outrage. Something may strike you and, if it does, I want to know about it right away.'

Both Dover and MacGregor looked considerably crestfallen when they heard what their role was to be. The thought of going over all that dreary old stuff yet again was enough to make hearts far stouter than theirs quail. However, needs must when a senior police officer drives, and the pair of them prepared to make the best of a bad job in their different ways.

MacGregor summed up his eager-beaver grin. 'You can rely on us, sir! We'll sift through everything with a fine tooth comb!'

'Yes,' agreed Dover through one of his enormous yawns. 'Leave it to us, eh? We'll get cracking on it first thing in the morning.'

'First thing in the morning, Dover? For God's sake, this is an emergency, man! You're to start *now*!'

'But we've had no bloody sleep!' whimpered Dover. ''Strewth, I haven't had my bloody head down for eighteen hours!'

'Come and see me when you haven't been to bed for eighteen days!' came the cruel rejoinder. 'Now, get moving!'

Thirteen

Another trouble with work was that it always went straight to Dover's stomach. The morning after the kidnapping of the Sleights's baby proved to be no exception and the chief inspector's forays down the corridor got steadily longer and more frequent. MacGregor, forced to remain behind holding the fort in the office, rightly suspected that Dover was taking the opportunity to snatch a quiet nap out there.

Endless cardboard cups of tasteless canteen coffee didn't help, either.

'Oh, 'strewth!' Dover pushed aside the bits of paper he'd been scribbling on and began extricating himself once more from behind his desk. 'Hospital's where I ought to be, not sitting here sweating my guts out! Ooh,' – he turned to MacGregor in the hope of halving his troubles – 'it feels like having your tripes twisted by somebody's cold hands!'

MacGregor suppressed a little frisson of distaste. 'Really, sir?'

Dover had reached the door. 'Back in a couple of shakes!' he promised bravely.

MacGregor got up and stretched his legs. He looked at his watch. Half past eleven, and they'd been at it since three. God, it was turning out to be a long, hard morning. MacGregor gave himself a break and, still trying to ease the ache in his back, wandered around emptying ashtrays. The air was thick with smoke and, in defiance of regulations designed to cut the cost of the central heating, he opened a window and let the sharp, spring zephyrs come whistling in. Soon be Easter, he thought, apropos of absolutely nothing. He started tidying up the papers on his desk, straightening the files dealing with Dover's kidnapping and sweeping the screwed up bits of scribble paper into the waste-paper basket.

There was still no sign of Dover returning.

MacGregor, giving his passion for neatness a field day, moved over and prepared to deal with the shambles on the desk of his lord and master. There was ash everywhere – over the toffee papers and the disposable coffee cups and the spent matches and . . . MacGregor went and got the duster out that he kept in his desk drawer. Ugh, talk about a pig sty ! The scraps of paper on which Dover had been doodling presented more of a problem than the other items of useless rubbish and MacGregor gave them a perfunctory glance before chucking them away. The results of Dover's long hours of work were revealing. Several sheets of paper had apparently been devoted to handwriting practice and were covered with Dover's name and address in a variety of styles and scripts. Then there was the Art section. Animal studies. Very, very long dachshund type dogs alternating with crude representations of cats made up of two circles, two ears, whiskers and a tail. MacGregor sighed. You'd get better from a pre-school play-group of slow learners ! He slung the dogs and cats into the waste-paper basket after the calligraphy and picked up the next sheet. For a moment he couldn't quite make out what it was. He had to turn the paper round several times before he got it. That uncertain scrawl wandering from top to bottom of the paper was a large capital B. Once you'd spotted that, the rest of the writing – adminton, ristol and ath – slotted neatly into place. Dover had just laboriously noted down the names of three of the towns

155

which had figured, however peripherally, in his abduction. Badminton, Bristol and Bath. MacGregor placed the paper precisely in the middle of Dover's now denuded desk. It must have been the alliteration that had taken the old fool's fancy.

MacGregor shook his duster out of the window and folded it thoughtfully.

Or was it ? That was the trouble with Dover. You never knew whether he was wandering in his wits or whether he really had got hold of something. If there was one thing that really got up MacGregor's nose, it was being out-smarted by an illiterate slob like Dover. Just in case this was liable to happen again, the sergeant began to rack his brains. Badminton – now, that was where Archie Gallagher, the public school bigamist, had been arrested and Bath was where the Claret Tapper girl, Mary Jones, had bought her blue suede jacket. And the third one ? MacGregor moved back to Dover's desk to refresh his memory about the third town and was thus caught red-handed when the chief inspector burst into the room. Dover's speed was the result of his mistaken impression that Commander Brockhurst was after him, but that particular terror was forgotten when he saw MacGregor hovering round his desk.

'What the hell are you doing there?' he roared, leaping across the room, grabbing his piece of paper and clutching it protectively to his manly chest. 'And shut that bloody window !'

MacGregor meekly complied with this last instruction. 'I was just tidying things up a bit, sir.'

'You were spying !' snarled Dover, pointing an accusing and dirty finger. 'Sneaking around trying to pinch all my ideas ! Judas !'

'Oh, nonsense, sir !' MacGregor's attempt to laugh the whole thing off was a dismal failure.

'It's not nonsense !' insisted Dover, unpeeling the sheet of paper from his chest and having a quick squint at it to see what was so important. He found himself at even more of a loss than MacGregor had been. 'You work out your own bloody theories,' he growled, 'and stop trying to nick mine!' 'Strewth,' he added disgustedly, 'it comes to something when you can't even trust your own bloody sergeant.'

'Sir,' said MacGregor, holding firmly onto his temper, 'I was simply tidying up – emptying the ashtrays and so on. In any case, you and I are hardly rivals, are we, sir? We are not competing to see who can solve the case first. We're supposed to be working as a team and pooling our ideas, if any.'

'So you say!' grumbled Dover, eyeing MacGregor thoughtfully. Nobody knew better than Dover that even the most brilliant detective needed somebody to do the donkey work for him. He decided to trust his sergeant – well, a bit of the way, at any rate. 'It's just that it suddenly struck me, you see.' He sat down at his desk and straightened his piece of paper out.

'What suddenly struck you, sir?' asked MacGregor encouragingly.

Dover had actually got his mouth open to tell him when the door burst open again. 'Excuse me, sir, but Commander Brockhurst wants to see you and Sergeant MacGregor in his office right away!'

Dover's mouth remained in the gaping position. 'Why didn't he use the bloody telephone?' he asked, wondering if there was some new directive about economising on phone calls that he'd missed.

The young messenger grinned. 'The operators are having a work-to-rule, sir, so it's quicker to walk. You won't forget that Commander Brockhurst is waiting, will you, sir?'

Commander Brockhurst was not so much waiting as hopping about like a cat on hot bricks. This time the courtesies were dispensed with and Dover and MacGregor were not asked to sit down. The commander came straight to the point. 'We've heard from the Claret Tappers again!'

Much to MacGregor's relief, Dover didn't ask who the Claret Tappers were. No doubt personal involvement had improved the old fool's memory. 'Another telephone message,

157

sir?' asked MacGregor, doing his bright young neophyte act.

'Yes. The cheeky buggers phoned the London Library this time. If there's one thing I can't stand,' said Commander Brockhurst with considerable venom, 'it's crooks with a sense of humour. Anyhow, we got a detailed description of the baby's bootees to prove that we're dealing with the real McCoy. They're very sharp this lot, you know. I wouldn't be surprised if we weren't dealing with a bunch of smart-alec, left-wing university students after all. Anyhow, they reiterated their demand for half a million pounds ransom and added the release of no less than six child murderers from Broadmoor. How sick can you get, eh?'

'Six child murderers from Broadmoor?' echoed MacGregor in tones of horror.

'Loonies?' queried Dover. ''Strewth, you can't release a bunch of criminal nutcases, can you? Specially not when they've been locked up for killing kids. The general public'll go berserk.'

'And what do you think the Prime Minister's going to do if we don't get that kid back?' demanded Commander Brockhurst sourly. 'The way I hear it, he's prepared to hand over the crown jewels, never mind release a few social misfits. What I can't fathom is why in God's name the Claret Tappers should want six homicidal maniacs let loose in the first place.'

'As a distraction, sir?' suggested MacGregor. 'On the grounds that we'll be so busy trying to recapture the Broadmoor lot that we'll not have time to go chasing after the kidnappers?'

'Could be,' said Commander Brockhurst. He was looking very tired. 'They've laid down another condition. The ransom money is to be paid over by Chief Inspector Dover.'

Dover's interest in the proceedings, which had been wandering just a little, came snapping back. 'Me?' he yelled indignantly. 'Why me, for God's sake? Look, I've done my whack and more! This kidnapping's damn all to do with me. Besides, I'm not fit. I've only been struggling on this long just to oblige. By rights I ought to be lying on a sick bed and . . .'

'*Listen, Dover !*' Commander Brockhurst slashed through the cackle with head-reeling brutality. 'If the Claret Tappers want you to hand over the ransom money, then that's it and no bloody argument ! Understand ? They're calling the tune at the moment and we've no choice but to dance to it. None of us like it, but some of us are just going to have to make a few sacrifices.'

Dover's jowls wobbled. 'I don't remember anybody making any bloody sacrifices for me when I was the kidnap victim !' he pointed out with considerable justice. 'Sink or swim – that's what they told me. Hard luck, mate – that's all the help I got. 'Strewth, I can't remember anybody raising so much as a finger to save my bloody skin !'

This was getting far too close to home for Commander Brockhurst's comfort. He turned to MacGregor. 'Get him down to Salisbury on the first available train. You go with him. When you get to Salisbury you're to put up at an hotel called The Bishop's Crozier and wait for further instructions. You'll liaise with a Superintendent Trevelyan of the local police. Got it ?'

MacGregor nodded. 'I take it that this move to Salisbury is in compliance with the kidnappers' instructions, sir ?'

'Well, you don't think I bloody well made it up, do you ?'

MacGregor generously overlooked this tetchy outburst. 'Is somebody going on television again, sir, to tell the Claret Tappers that we're accepting their demands ?'

Commander Brockhurst shook his head. 'The joker who rang up the London Library just now said that acceptance of their terms was a foregone conclusion and there was no need to make any arrangements for letting them know our answer.' He sighed. 'He was right, of course. Until we get that kid back, when the Claret Tappers say jump, we are going to jump. I suppose you didn't come up with any new leads about Chief Inspector Dover's kidnapping ? No, I thought not. Well, there it is. For the time being we've no choice but to play it the Claret

159

Tappers' way.'

Dover rested his weight on the edge of Commander Brockhurst's desk. 'Are we really going to hand over half a million quid ?' he asked, looking happier as he got seventeen and a quarter stone off his feet. 'And whose money is it, if it comes to that ? The bloody taxpayers', I suppose. Me,' – he settled down for a cosy chat – 'I can't see what all the fuss is about. I mean – the Prime Minister's daughter's still a young woman, isn't she ?'

'What,' interrupted Commander Brockhurst fiercely, 'the hell has that to do with anything ?'

Dover looked mildly surprised at the question. 'Only that she's got bags of time to have a dozen more brats if she wants 'em,' he explained. 'I mean,' – he chuckled a man-to-man sort of chuckle – 'it's not all that difficult, is it ?'

The jaws of Commander Brockhurst came together like a vice and it was clear that he didn't trust himself to speak.

Luckily Dover wasn't in the least bit sensitive to atmospheres. He made himself even more comfortable on the desk. 'Still, you know me ! A hundred per cent effort no matter what I think of the personalities involved. And, provided I get a bit of decent support from my so-called colleagues, I don't doubt we'll bring the whole thing to a successful conclusion. Sooner or later.'

Commander Brockhurst's face went a very peculiar shade of red. Those iron jaws unclamped and his head turned slightly in MacGregor's direction. 'Get him out of here !'

The Bishop's Crozier was not the worst hotel in Salisbury. The Old Ram had a much more fearsome reputation and it was rather surprising that the Claret Tappers hadn't condemned Dover to await their summons there. Maybe it was the unique location of The Bishop's Crozier which had tipped the scales as there are not many provincial hotels which share a noisy cul-de-sac with an all-night fish and chip shop, a small glue factory and a house of ill repute.

' 'Strewth !' said Dover, looking round the double room

which he was condemned to share with MacGregor. 'What a dump !'

MacGregor was even more distressed at the prospect which lay before them and had, indeed, only bowed to the inevitable after a long argument with mine host about the impossibility of providing a second room. If there was one thing MacGregor did like, it was his privacy. 'Which bed do you want, sir ?'

'I'll have the one by the door,' said Dover, predictably. 'Just in case I get taken short during the night.' He continued with his unpacking, putting his tin of stomach powder on the shelf over the wash-basin. 'How long are we supposed to be stopping here ?'

MacGregor shook his head. 'Nobody knows, sir. Until the Claret Tappers get in touch again with the next set of instructions, I suppose. I shouldn't think it would be very long.'

Dover sullenly dropped his spare pair of socks in the dressing-table drawer. They were the only spare clothes he'd brought with him and he didn't want them to come to any harm. 'It could be bloody weeks,' he said, feeling in an argumentative mood.

'Oh, I don't think so, sir.' MacGregor smoothed his blue suit lovingly under its plastic cover and hung it carefully in the wardrobe. 'Every minute this goes on makes it more dangerous for the kidnappers. A three-month-old baby takes a lot of looking after and the sooner they can get rid of it, the happier they'll be.'

'Always provided they haven't already knocked it on the head,' said Dover.

'Even if they have, sir, they still won't want to drag things out. They'll want that money in their hands and then a quick get-away.'

'Half a million ?' said Dover incredulously. 'They've a hope.'

MacGregor didn't like to be continually correcting Dover, but he didn't often have much choice. 'Actually, sir, it's already here and waiting.'

161

'What is ?'

MacGregor reduced his voice to a whisper. 'The money, sir. The five hundred thousand pounds.'

'Get off !' Dover's piggy little eyes grew round with greed. 'Where is it ? Have you got it ?' He looked hopefully round the bedroom. MacGregor always carted such a load of clobber round with him that he might well have half a million nicker tucked away in the odd . . .

'It's in one of the cellars, sir. Under armed guard. Commander Brockhurst reckons that, when the Claret Tappers do get in touch, we shall have to respond to their instructions very quickly. They'll only give us the bare minimum of time so that we can't organise a trap for them.'

'What's all this "we" business ?' demanded Dover crossly. 'I'm the poor devil that's going to be out there in the firing line, laddie, and don't you forget it. Here,' – what little colour there was drained from his podgy face – 'you don't think they'll grab me again and hold me as hostage, do you ?'

MacGregor couldn't imagine anybody being that masochistic and his attempts to reassure the craven Dover had the ring of truth about them.

Dover was quick to cash in on his sergeant's sympathy. 'Let's go downstairs and have a drink,' he suggested, swinging his feet off the eiderdown and planting them heavily on the floor.

But MacGregor had to knock this bright idea on the head as Commander Brockhurst had given strict instructions that Dover was to maintain a low profile and keep out of sight. The press and television boys were now on to the kidnapping and the Home Secretary himself had held a briefing during which he had appealed for discretion and restraint. Only the barest facts had been revealed, just that the baby grandson of the Prime Minister had been kidnapped and that the au pair girl looking after him had been killed. Nothing was said about the release of the child murderers from Broadmoor, the demand for half a million pounds, or that the Claret Tappers were claiming responsibility for the baby's abduction. Nothing had been said, either, about the involvement of Chief Inspector Dover in the handing over of the money. As Commander Brockhurst had observed unkindly – there was enough misery in this world without needlessly adding to it.

'I'll pop down and fetch you a drink up, sir,' said MacGregor when he'd finished explaining why Dover couldn't make a personal appearance in the bar of The Bishop's Crozier.

Dover flopped back on the bed, his filthy boots once more sinking into the long-suffering eiderdown. 'All right,' he agreed in a disconsolate whine, 'but it's not the same, you know.'

At six o'clock in the morning, the Claret Tappers struck. They phoned their orders through to the switchboard of the local maternity hospital and there was some delay before the message was relayed to the police. Superintendent Trevelyan, a large placid man who could see his pension and country cottage at the end of the tunnel, woke MacGregor and readily acquiesced to his suggestion that they should let the sleeping Dover lie until they had worked out their strategy.

'Not that he's going to get much more than an extra twenty minutes,' said Superintendent Trevelyan as they made their way quietly down the stairs. 'We've got to get him to the foot of Fish Down by half past seven. Still, that shouldn't take us more than twenty minutes at this time in the morning.'

They settled down in the chilly saloon bar. It reeked of stale tobacco smoke and spilt beer. MacGregor wrapped his vicuna dressing-gown more closely round him as he studied the sheet of paper which the superintendent had handed him. 'Well, it looks straightforward enough, sir. We've just got to get Mr Dover to the bottom of Fish Down with the money at seven thirty. There, he'll find further instructions. If the police attempt to interfere or follow the collectors of the money in any way, the kidnapped child will be killed. "We are not fooling, pigs. Signed: The Claret Tappers."' MacGregor stifled a yawn. 'Pretty much what we expected, sir.'

Superintendent Trevelyan agreed. 'We shall try and follow

'em, of course. We've had orders from on high about that. It's going to be tricky, though.' He unfolded a large-scale Ordnance Survey map. 'Fish Down's right in the middle of the Plain, you see. No cover. And I don't see how we can make any form of transport look inconspicuous at that time in the morning.' He tapped the map with his finger. 'There are half a dozen roads we ought to cover, in both directions.'

MacGregor stared. 'Fish Down looks like the centre of quite a little complex of roads, sir. I suppose that's why they chose it. A car could come along from any direction and pick up the money and clear off in almost any direction again.' He scratched his head. 'An army helicopter, sir?'

'Well, we've always got them buzzing around over the Plain, of course, but I think one over Fish Down this morning would look jolly suspicious. As a matter of fact, I've already sent a request to the Army to keep clear till midday.' The superintendent felt obliged to justify his decision. 'We've got to remember that child's safety, you know. The Claret Tappers' threats are quite clear. If they spot any police involvement, they'll kill.'

'The way you're talking, sir,' said MacGregor rather highhandedly, 'it sounds as though you think we shouldn't be maintaining any surveillance at all.'

'I don't think we should,' said Superintendent Trevelyan flatly. 'I reckon we're putting that baby's life in jeopardy by even sitting here discussing it. However, I'm only an executive officer in this operation, chosen for my local knowledge. The orders are coming from London.'

MacGregor looked at the map again. 'How do you propose to tackle the problem, sir?'

Superintendent Trevelyan consulted the sheet of paper he'd taken out of his briefcase. 'Well, it's been a bit of a rush job, as you can imagine, but I propose sticking one chap in mufti up here on Caper Hill with a pair of binoculars and a radio. We're lucky that the only other hill in the area besides Fish Down covers this same complex of roads. My chap should be able to

164

spot the pick-up with no trouble at all.'

'And he'll then radio a description of the kidnappers' vehicle and the direction they're taking?'

'That's about it. I'll have cars concealed along these roads where I can. There's a couple of farmyards we can use and this little coppice here might provide a bit of shelter. Always providing the Claret Tappers themselves aren't using it,' the superintendent added despondently. 'If the pick-up doesn't take place immediately, though, we stand a bit better chance because there'll be more traffic about as the morning draws on. I'll be able to infiltrate a few more of my lads without arousing too much suspicion.'

'Not in police cars, sir, I hope?' MacGregor didn't really trust the intelligence of people who lived in the country from choice.

'No, sergeant,' said Superintendent Trevelyan heavily, '*not* in police cars.'

MacGregor hurriedly found a new topic of conversation. 'How do you envisage the hand-over of the money, sir? Do you think Mr Dover will just have to dump it by the side of the road and then drive off, leaving the Claret Tappers to come along and pick it up at their leisure? Or will there be an actual, physical hand-over, with the chief inspector having to hang about until they turn up?' MacGregor sighed. 'He won't like that, I'm afraid.'

Superintendent Trevelyan looked at his watch. 'Time's getting on,' he warned. 'I think we should be waking your boss pretty soon. I've asked the landlord if he can't lay on a bit of breakfast before we set out. It's pretty parky outside. The hand-over?' The superintendent ran a hand over his stubbly chin. 'Have you considered the possibility that the contact might already be in position? There's a bit of cover on Fish Down – bushes and what-not. One of the Claret Tappers could well have concealed himself there before they even sent the telephone message.'

'Ready to jump out when Mr Dover arrives?' MacGregor

looked very unhappy. 'He'll have a heart attack.'

'Or they might shoot him,' said Superintendent Trevelyan, obviously one of nature's optimists.

'Why on earth should they?' asked MacGregor in a rather hoarse voice. 'I mean, surely they don't think they're in any danger from him?'

You could see that Superintendent Trevelyan wasn't the sort of man who lay awake at nights worrying. 'They might think Chief Inspector Dover has a two-way radio on him,' he observed stolidly, 'and was going to use it to communicate with a police net spread over the countryside to shadow the kidnappers to their lair.'

MacGregor picked up the piece of paper containing the plan of operations and tried to match the superintendent's detached approach. 'But I thought it had been agreed that Mr Dover *would* be carrying a two-way radio concealed about his person, sir?'

'That's right, sergeant.'

Fourteen

The best laid plans of mice and men can rarely stand up to the Dovers of this world. At first glance it looked as though the Claret Tappers had allowed for every eventuality. Chief Inspector Dover was to drive to the foot of Fish Down, arriving there at exactly half-past seven. He was to be alone in the car and was to be carrying the ransom money (in used notes, of course) in two large canvas bags of the kind used by postmen. When he arrived at Fish Down, Dover was to keep his eyes skinned for further instructions. Nobody was to accompany Dover or to follow him or, indeed, attempt to meddle in the operation in any way. Failure to comply with this instruction would mean the death of the kidnapped child.

It was all brutally simple and direct.

Apart from Dover's natural reluctance to expose himself to exertion and danger, there was however one major snag.

Superintendent Trevelyan – a novice where Dover was concerned – looked as though he couldn't believe his ears. 'You can't drive ?'

Dover was looking happier than he had since they woke him up. 'Reckon I might as well go back to bed, eh ?'

It soon became apparent that such a withdrawal was only

going to be achieved over the combined dead bodies of MacGregor and Superintendent Trevelyan, and Dover sulkily sat down again and finished off the toast and marmalade. There was by now very little time to spare and solutions to this latest problem began being scattered around like leaves in an autumn gale.

Once Dover had accepted the fact that he wasn't going to be allowed to take the easy way out, he too joined in the fun. His most sensible suggestion came out in a spray of toast crumbs. 'MacGregor can go disguised as me ! If he wears my bowler and overcoat, his own mother wouldn't recognise him !'

'He'd need a bit of padding,' said Superintendent Trevelyan, prepared at this stage to give almost any idea a fair hearing.

MacGregor's gorge had risen at the prospect of donning those unspeakable garments. Dear God – not all the perfumes of Arabia would sweeten him after that ! 'You forget that the Claret Tappers have already seen you, sir,' he pointed out quickly. 'My impersonation wouldn't survive two seconds at close quarters.'

'Chicken !' sneered Dover.

Superintendent Trevelyan made up his mind. 'You'll have to drive the car to the foot of Fish Down, sergeant,' he said. 'You can drop Chief Inspector Dover with the ransom money and then drive off.'

'And leave me stranded there ?' howled Dover.

'You'll both have two-way radios,' explained the superintendent patiently. 'It'll be the easiest thing in the world to call him back if you want him. No !' He held up his hand with real authority. 'I know it's not perfect but it'll have to do. We haven't got time to work out anything better. Now, are you ready, Dover ? Good ! We've got your car waiting outside. It's filled right up with petrol, by the way, in case you've got to go driving half-way over the country. The ransom money's already in the car and . . . Where the hell are you off to now ?'

Dover was going to the gents'. 'Shan't be a tick !' he said.

168

When, only a short time later, he found himself standing at the bottom of Fish Down watching MacGregor disappearing down the long rain-swept road, he was extremely glad he'd taken the opportunity when he'd had it. With the wind whistling round and only a couple of stunted bushes for cover, it'd be no bloody joke out here trying to . . .

His pocket radio crackled. 'Well ?' asked a distant voice.

'Well, what ?' riposted Dover after a lengthy pause while he found the right buttons and switches.

'Have you found a message or anything ?'

Dover sighed heavily as befits one who is being driven beyond the bounds of endurance and went to have a look round. He eventually found a red, plastic bag sticking out from under a stone. With some difficulty he undid it, extracted the sheet of paper it contained and began laboriously to read the typewritten instructions. His subsequent scream of horror almost reached the ears of his colleagues without benefit of radio.

'Jesus Christ!'

There was more delay before he got through again on the fiddly little wireless thing they'd given him. What with frustration and simple panic, he was almost sobbing when he finally got through.

'Don't shout !' advised the distant MacGregor, wondering if one of the Claret Tappers really had jumped out and shot the old fool. 'We can't make out what you're saying.'

Dover turned his back on the howling gale and reduced his voice to an anguished scream. 'They say I've got to take this bloody money up to the top of this bloody mountain !'

MacGregor and Superintendent Trevelyan had joined up and were sitting together in a warm and comfortable police car a couple of miles away. Superintendent Trevelyan took over the microphone. 'Well, that's all right, old chap,' he said soothingly. 'Just go ahead and do what they say !'

'Go ahead?' bellowed Dover. 'Have you gone out of your mind ? It's three bloody miles straight up, for God's sake ! And

169

these bags with the money – they weigh a bloody ton, you moron !'

Superintendent Trevelyan tried sweet reason. He tried some good-humoured banter. He appealed to Dover's finer feelings and spoke rather movingly about the poor kidnapped baby. Then came veiled threats which were quickly supplanted by naked threats. Finally, Superintendent Trevelyan took a deep breath and issued a direct order.

It was all to no avail. Dover continued to whine that the physical effort demanded by the kidnappers was totally beyond him.

In the end Superintendent Trevelyan laid it on the line. 'Listen, Dover,' he snarled, crushing his two-way radio in his fist, 'and get this into that thick skull of yours ! Either you carry that money up the green road to the top of Fish Down as per instructions or you stay out there until your bloody bones rot ! The choice is yours, mate ! A bit of a climb up a bit of a hill or death from exposure !'

'I'll sue you !' spluttered Dover. 'I'm a sick man ! My . . .'

'You may be interested to hear the latest weather forecast,' the implacable voice went on. 'A cold front preceded by a belt of heavy rain is moving slowly across the area. There's a likelihood of snow over high ground.'

Dover, in a paroxysm of rage, took the only course open to a man of his stomach and spirit. He chucked his radio away as far as he could and had the deep satisfaction of seeing it smash into a thousand pieces on the roadway. Much cheered by this display of petulance, he determined to stick it out and defiantly raised two gloved fingers to the lot of 'em !

Four and a half minutes of lashing rain, freezing gales and not a bloody car in sight changed his tune for him. With a heart-felt curse, he grabbed hold of his two mail-bags and staggered off up the hill, his feet stumbling over the stones and slipping desperately in the thick mud.

'What the hell d'you mean, you don't know what he's doing ?'

170

Everybody was having their difficulties. Superintendent Trevelyan and MacGregor, snug in their police car, couldn't see anything of what was going on at Fish Down. For information about that they had to rely on the man Superintendent Trevelyan had stationed with binoculars on the top of Caper Hill.

'Oh, I've got it now, sir !' The distant voice sounded happier. 'Chief Inspector Dover's carrying the bags one at a time.'

Superintendent Trevelyan was feeling the strain. 'How d'you mean ?' he demanded angrily. 'Carrying the bags one at a time ?'

The distant voice sounded hurt. 'Well, what I say, sir. Mr Dover's dropping one bag on the ground and carrying the other one fifty yards or so, dropping it to the ground and then going back for the other.'

Superintendent Trevelyan turned to and on MacGregor. 'It'll take him a month of Sundays to get to the top !'

MacGregor, knowing Dover better, thought that this was, if anything, an underestimation. 'There's nothing we can do about it, I'm afraid, sir. If that was his radio your chap saw him throw away . . .'

'I'll make him pay for that radio !' Superintendent Trevelyan promised himself and everybody else within earshot. 'Down to the last penny ! By God I will !' He clicked the switch of his own radio again. 'Where's the stup . . . Where's the chief inspector got to now ?'

The man on the top of Caper Hill sighed. 'Well, he's about where he was when you asked before, actually, sir. He's been taking a bit of a breather.'

But even all bad things come to an end sometime and Dover eventually, and somewhat to his surprise, reached the summit, disappearing as he did so out of the sight of the policeman watching from the other hill. When he had got his breath back he looked around for signs of the Claret Tappers and eventually found another brightly coloured plastic envelope anchored under a stone. Being Dover, he very nearly let the

171

enclosed missive blow away in the wind but he caught it, only slightly torn, just in time. The tears which sprang to his eyes when he'd finished reading the message were not due solely to the icy blast which was slicing its way across the summit of Fish Down. Bloody hell, was there no decency left in this bleeding world ? Dover let the kidnappers' instructions blow away to God knows where, and looked morosely about him for the next link in this accursed chain.

There it was !

Two malevolent eyes squinted suspiciously at him from under an untidy tuft of black, greasy hair. Powerful jaws ruminated maliciously as Dover extended a would-be conciliatory hand and, uncertainly, clicked his teeth.

The next link in the chain curled a green and slimy lip, and eyed the two mail-bags with misgiving.

'For the love of God, what's that damned fool doing now ?'

The watching policeman lowered his binoculars and flicked the transmitter switch. 'Chief Inspector Dover is still out of my line of vision, sir,' he reported impassively. 'He took cover a couple of minutes ago behind an outcrop of rock. No doubt he'll appear again when he's done whatever it is he's doing.'

MacGregor sensed rather than saw the exasperated twitch of Superintendent Trevelyan's eyebrows. 'Mr Dover's bladder isn't all it might be, sir,' he explained in a suitably hushed voice. 'He sometimes has - er - difficulties.'

Superintendent Trevelyan had a heart of stone. 'Bladder ?' he echoed fiercely. 'I'll bladder him all right if he mucks this up !'

The radio receiver crackled again and the watching policeman could be heard clearing his throat. 'Sir,' he said at last, well aware that he was on a hiding to nothing, 'there seems to be a - well - a sort of - er - *animal*, sir.'

Superintendent Trevelyan appeared to be trying to tie his swagger stick into a knot. 'Have you been drinking, laddie ?'

The watching policeman had no time to protest his innocence. 'It *is* an animal, sir !' he gabbled excitedly. 'I can see it

172

quite clearly now. A little Shetland pony. And it's got those mail-bags on its back, sir ! The mail-bags with the ransom money in them. It's trotting off down the side of the hill now, sir !'

'Northwards ?' MacGregor struggled with the large-scale Ordnance Survey map although he already appreciated the implications of the watching policeman's report. 'Oh, God – that's right away from the roads. Look, there aren't even cart tracks for miles in this direction. We haven't got it covered. We're not going to be able to follow!'

'Damn ! Damn ! Damn ! Damn !' Superintendent Trevelyan leaned forward as though the appearance of extreme urgency could in itself produce results. He clicked on his radio. 'Where is the blasted pony now ?'

'Sorry, sir,' – the watching policeman's disappointed tones came across loud and clear – 'it's already gone out of my sight. It was moving pretty fast, sir, in spite of those mail-bags.'

Superintendent Trevelyan pulled the map out of MacGregor's hands though he knew the surrounding countryside like the back of his hand. One irate glance was enough to confirm all his worst fears. That bloody pony, with half a million bloody quid on its back, could go for miles and miles and finish up anywhere. But the superintendent was not the man to cry over spilt milk. Firmly banishing the vision of those empty, rolling acres from his mind, he concentrated on the one aspect of the problem which really counted. 'Somebody,' he announced grimly in a way that left no doubt but that he was excluding himself from the calculation, 'is going to answer with his head for this bloody balls-up !'

At the acrimonious de-briefing session which was held some couple of hours later, it became clear that Dover was the one being groomed for the role of sacrificial victim. Everybody concerned was gathered in the saloon bar of The Bishop's Crozier for the dismal purpose of mulling over what had gone wrong. The air was thick with smoke and recriminations as the hot potatoes of this particular disaster were tossed recklessly

173

from hand to hand. Gradually, however, the pattern of Superintendent Trevelyan's bandwaggon began to emerge and his
immediate underlings lost no time in jumping thankfully
aboard. After all, dog traditionally does not eat dog, and men of
the same police force do have a certain loyalty to each other.
Much better to shove all the blame onto these toffee-nosed
buggers from Scotland Yard. Well – let's be fair – it was probably all their bleeding fault, anyhow.

'Just a bloody minute !' Up to this point in the proceedings
Dover had been worrying mostly about his feet, his stomach
and his bowels. Now he suddenly became preoccupied with his
skin. Holy flaming cats – these thick-headed, straw-chewing
yokels were trying to frame him ! 'All I was supposed to do was
to hand that ransom money over to the Claret Tappers and
that's all I did. It's not my fault that your damned stupid
arrangements blew up in your silly faces.'

'You shouldn't have thrown that radio away !' countered the
superintendent, who was nothing if not consistent.

'And you shouldn't have underestimated the Claret
Tappers !' retorted Dover. 'A kid of two'd know they wouldn't
stick to the main roads just so's you could keep an eye on 'em.'
He raised his voice on the grounds that the best means of
defence is often shouting. 'They're not a bunch of country
bumpkins, you know !'

Superintendent Trevelyan, on the other hand, belonged
more to the constant dripping school. 'If you hadn't tossed that
valuable radio away, you could have tipped us off and we'd
have had time to organise something. It's entirely thanks to
your bungling that the Claret Tappers slipped clean through
our fingers – and I shall be putting that in my report to my
Chief Constable.' He broke off as the door into the bar opened
and a rather oily young man came sidling into the room. 'Well,'
demanded Superintendent Trevelyan as the newcomer paused obsequiously in front of him, 'has the Prime Minister's
grandson been returned ?'

The face of the oily young man fell. The news he was bearing was interesting and important, but not as interesting and important as *that*. Blimey, some people wanted it with jam on ! 'There's no news about the Sleight baby, sir,' he said. 'We've found the Shetland pony, though.'

Dover was not the man to let a chunk of bathos like that fall unnoticed. 'Oh, big deal !' he guffawed, thumping MacGregor in the ribs to encourage him to appreciate the joke.

The oily young man blinked but carried on gallantly. 'The pony belongs to a Captain Berry, sir, up over at a place called Gallows Farm.' He indicated the spot on the large wall map which some helpful bastard had hung up over the dart board. 'It's about three miles from where Mr Dover released the animal, sir, at the top of Fish Down. Three miles as the crow flies, of course, sir.'

'And not as the pony trots !' sniggered Dover, giving his natural wit full rein.

Superintendent Trevelyan went quite red in the face. 'Well, get on with it !' he snarled at the oily young man who was standing with his mouth wide open.

'Eh ? Oh, yes – er – yes, of course, sir. Well, we've only got the report of the local constable so far, sir, but it seems that Captain Berry reckons the pony was taken sometime last night. The captain thought he heard somebody moving around later on in the paddock but he didn't get up to investigate. He says there'd be no trouble in luring the pony away because it's a greedy little brute and would go off with Old Nick himself for a couple of carrots. That's why it shot off home like a bat out of hell as soon as Mr Dover untied it, sir. It wanted its breakfast. Captain Berry says it returned home just before eight this morning, sir, and – and apart from looking a bit bedraggled and cross – it didn't seem to have come to any harm. It . . .'

'What about the money ?' Superintendent Trevelyan wasn't much of an animal lover at the best of times.

The oily young man blinked again. 'Oh, there's no sign of the money, sir,' he assured the superintendent earnestly. 'Police Constable Truss – he's the one we got this report from, sir – he thinks the kidnappers must have waited for the pony at the gate to its paddock. There are some indications that several people may have been standing round about there and there might have been a car, too. The trouble is that with all this rain it's difficult to be sure about anything much. Presumably, when the pony came trotting home, sir, the kidnappers just grabbed it, removed the sacks containing the ransom money and . . .'

'Get out !' Superintendent Trevelyan liked to think he was a father to his men – but not this morning.

'Half-way to South America by now !' observed Dover with quite unseemly cheerfulness.

'If they are, Dover, it's your bloody fault ! If you hadn't thrown that radio . . .'

MacGregor was as weary, anxious and disappointed as anybody but he tried to remember that he was a policeman, too. 'At least this ploy with the Shetland pony does give us a bit of a clue, doesn't it, sir ?'

Dover and Superintendent Trevelyan temporarily postponed their eyeball-to-eyeball confrontation. 'A clue ?'

MacGregor was a skilled hand when it came to explaining the painfully obvious to his superiors. He tapped the wall map. 'This Gallows Farm is miles from anywhere. How did the kidnappers know that there was a pony there, one they could get hold of and one upon whose homing instincts they could rely ?'

Superintendent Trevelyan chewed the end of his swagger stick. 'The Claret Tappers are local villains ? Is that what you're getting at ?'

'At least they have access to local knowledge, sir. It's worth following up, don't you think ? There can't be all that many people who would know about the pony, or the suitability of Fish Down for their scheme, if it comes to that.'

Unlike Dover, Superintendent Trevelyan was a man of action and, relieved to have something to do at last, began firing off orders like a runaway machine gun. All around, policemen and policewomen jumped to obey. There was a brief respite when the oily young man returned to convey yet another report. The Archbishop of Canterbury had received a telephone message from a man purporting to be a member of the Claret Tapper gang. The six designated child murderers were to be taken to the Isle of Anglesey immediately and set free in the well-known village of Llanfairpwllgwyngyllgogerychwyrndrobwillllantysiliogogoch.

As the oily young man fought his way to the end of his tidings, one of the young policewomen began to giggle hysterically. It was the chance that her sergeant, a much less nubile young woman, had been waiting for and the sound of the resulting smack echoed round the bar.

Superintendent Trevelyan seemed to be taking each fresh disaster personally. He raised his swagger stick to heaven. 'Dear God,' he moaned, 'it's getting more and more like a nightmare every minute! Isn't there any news of the Prime Minister's grandchild yet?'

The oily young man looked annoyed. Good God, if there had been, he'd have said, wouldn't he? 'If we've got to wait until they've released these degenerate psychopaths, sir, it'll be late this afternoon before we can hope to have any sort of word.'

Over in his corner, under the advertisement for milk stout, Dover was beginning to show all the classical signs of restlessness. It had been a long day and, with the ash from one of MacGregor's cigarettes dribbling unheeded down his waistcoat, the chief inspector's massive brow was crinkled in thought. Under the cover of the noise and confusion that Superintendent Trevelyan was generating, he turned petulantly to MacGregor. 'Isn't it time for lunch yet?'

Patiently MacGregor indicated the large clock on the wall in front of them. 'It's only a quarter past eleven, sir.'

Dover belched. ''Strewth, I could eat a horse!'

MacGregor couldn't think of any telling rejoinder to this, so he kept his mouth shut.

'I've been up since bloody crack of dawn!'

177

'I'm afraid it's just one of those days, sir.'

But Dover was in no mood to be comforted by mere words. As unobtrusively as possible for a man of his unwieldy girth, he got to his feet. 'Tell 'em to send me up a plate of sandwiches and a couple of pies!'

'For lunch, sir?'

'For now, you fool!'

MacGregor expressed some surprise that Dover was withdrawing from the fray.

'Not much bloody point in hanging round here,' grumbled Dover. 'With everybody rushing around like a bunch of chickens with their heads cut off. What I want is somewhere with a bit of peace and quiet where I can *think.*' He caught the expression of acute scepticism as it flickered across MacGregor's face. 'Well, it's about time somebody thought a bit, isn't it?' he demanded crossly. 'Actually,' – he began to manoeuvre over to the door – 'I've got a feeling we've missed something somewhere. Overlooked it, you know.'

MacGregor managed to stay just this side of insolence. 'Really, sir?'

'Yes, *really*!' snapped Dover. 'And it's about time you pulled your finger out and got down to some work, laddie! I'll have all the files relating to this bloody kidnapping lark up in my room in five minutes! Got it? With the sandwiches!'

By the time MacGregor eventually got upstairs with the cold collation and what few papers he could find relating to anything, Dover was already reclining once more on top of his bed. He dragged himself into a sitting position as MacGregor handed over the pile of sandwiches and dropped the papers on to where Dover's lap would have been if his paunch hadn't ousted it.

'Wassat?'

'The papers you asked for, sir.'

'Oh, yes.' Dover was more interested in examining the contents of the top sandwich. Sardine and beetroot! Good-oh! He let the upper layer of bread sink back into its place and glanced

178

up enquiringly at MacGregor. 'You waiting for a bloody bus, laddie?'

MacGregor fought down the oft-recurring impulse to ram the old lout's National Health dentures straight down his throat. 'I thought you might like to know, sir, that the Assistant Commissioner is coming down here. By helicopter. They're expecting him about two o'clock.'

'Order me an early lunch, then!' quipped Dover, quick as a flash.

'Apparently there's a high-level conference going on in London, sir,' MacGregor went on. 'The Home Secretary called it. It seems he's not best pleased with the way things have turned out.'

'And he's not the only one!' said Dover sanctimoniously. 'This whole case has been mishandled right from the bloody beginning. If some people had taken *my* kidnapping a bit more seriously, we shouldn't be in the mess we're in now. Anyhow,' – Sandwich Number Three was excavated – 'you shove off now, laddie, and leave me to sort things out.' He grasped a sheaf of papers in a greasy hand and waved them vaguely in the air. 'I've got some thinking to do, eh?'

'I'll give you a call at a quarter to one, sir.' MacGregor failed to resist the temptation to be slightly malicious. 'Just in case you get so engrossed that you forget what time it is.'

Fifteen

It will come as no surprise to either of Dover's fans that the chief inspector was flat out and snoring when MacGregor came tramping upstairs to break the glad tidings that lunch was ready. True, it was apparently going to consist of steak and kidney pudding with Spotted Dick for afters, but this wouldn't worry Dover, who preferred quantity to quality where food was concerned.

MacGregor had been having a rough time with Superintendent Trevelyan who still wanted somebody's guts for garters and would make do with a sergeant's if he couldn't get his hands on a chief inspector's. The noise at times in the bar parlour had been unbearable as twenty or thirty sweating coppers all shouted at each other at once. MacGregor paused wearily in the comparative peace and quiet of Dover's bedroom and reflected that he must be getting old. He just couldn't take the strain like he used to.

In order to give himself a few more seconds respite before rousing the worst bellower of the lot, MacGregor began tidying things up again. This mania for neatness was starting to get the better of him. He picked up the sandwich plate from the floor and noted that it had almost certainly been licked clean.

The bed, on the other hand, looked like the centre of a paper chase and MacGregor indulged in a little sigh of self-pity as he tried to restore some semblance of order to files which had been immaculate before Dover got his grubby paws on them.

And – oh dear ! – he'd been scribbling again. That was funny because, usually, Dover only put pen to paper at gun-point. Maybe he was suffering from insomnia? The stentorian grunts, snorts and bubbling coming from the bed would appear to negate that idea and MacGregor returned to wasting some time which he could ill afford examining the scraps of paper. What in heaven's name was this one ? Either a drawing of a middle-aged housewife in her curlers or the portrait of one of Her Majesty's High Court judges in wig and gown. Then there was another example of Dover's obsession with – appropriately enough – the letter B. Bristol, Badminton and Bath written several times in several equally unformed scripts. MacGregor sighed again. Talk about having your mind in a groove ! And what was this ? He turned the paper round on the off-chance that he was looking at this final effort upside down.

He was !

Why, the dirty-minded old lecher !

MacGregor had been very nicely brought up and was still, in spite of his gruelling years in the police, something of a mother's boy. It didn't take all that much to bring a blush to his cheek, especially where people of Dover's advanced age and senility were concerned. Activities and inclinations which MacGregor found perfectly natural in his contemporaries became unbelievably obscene when they were associated with his elders. To think that a worm-eaten old slob like Dover should even know about . . . much less *draw* it !

MacGregor, with a moue of prudish disgust, screwed the piece of paper up into a ball and flung it into the corner of the room. A split second later, he found himself following it. Hitting the wall with a most agonising crash, he discovered that his all-to-natural cries of pain and protest were being trapped in his throat as a forearm of steel slammed across his Adam's apple.

Exerting all his strength, MacGregor tried to shove Dover off.

The whole incident was, as a matter of fact, an interesting illustration of the perversity of human nature. Dover, who was quite capable of sleeping peacefully through the combined efforts of Armageddon and the Last Trump, had on this occasion been roused to violence by the mere crumpling of a piece of paper.

It was some time before either party recovered from the encounter. Dover didn't seem to know where he was, and MacGregor's throat was too bruised for speech.

'What did you do that for?' croaked MacGregor when, eventually, he'd got his voice back.

Dover sank down on the bed. 'You shouldn't have come creeping up on me like a thief in the night,' he complained. 'You know I've got these razor-sharp reactions.'

'Actually, sir,' said MacGregor, trying to massage some feeling back into his neck, 'I'd been standing there for some minutes.'

Dover stopped scratching his stomach. 'Doing what?' he demanded with all the old suspicions bubbling up.

'I just came upstairs to wake you, sir.'

'Wasn't asleep!' snapped Dover, just to keep the record straight.

'The Assistant Commissioner's helicopter's already landed, sir. He should be here in about ten minutes.'

''Strewth!' Dover rushed over to the wash-basin and freshened up by rinsing his false teeth under the cold water tap. 'Here, wath abouth my lunth?'

'The Assistant Commissioner wants everybody to attend a working luncheon, sir.'

'A working luncheon?' echoed Dover miserably as he munched his dentures back into place. 'Don't they know what that sort of thing does to my digestion. 'Strewth, I'll have the bloody cramps for a week. Here,' – his eye alighted on the piece

182

of paper that MacGregor had thrown away in disgust – 'what's happened to my notes ?'

'Your notes, sir ?' MacGregor retrieved the paper and flattened it out. 'I'm sorry. I thought it was just scrap paper.'

'Ho, did you ?' Dover could tell when somebody was being sarcastic and he didn't like it. 'It may interest you to know, laddie, that I've all but solved this bloody case.'

Of course Dover hadn't solved the case and MacGregor knew he hadn't. And Dover knew that MacGregor knew he hadn't. Which knowledge merely drove the chief inspector to more and more extravagant claims backed up by wild talk about the paucity of the loose ends that still needed to be tied up.

MacGregor remained sceptical. 'I suppose you're talking about the three B's again, sir,' he said patronisingly.

Dover was indignant. 'Paul Pry !'

'Bristol, Bath and Badminton !' MacGregor chuckled indulgently. 'I don't quite see how they're going to solve all our problems, sir. What's significant about them, may one ask ? Apart from the fact that they all begin with the same letter, of course.'

'You'll laugh on the other side of your silly face,' snarled Dover, every chin quivering with indignation, 'when those towns turn out to be the key to this whole bloody business !' He was standing in front of the dressing-table mirror, smartening himself up for his encounter with the Assistant Commissioner.

MacGregor, for whom elegance was almost a religion, watched Dover trying to flatten his hair out with spit and picking the flakes of dandruff out of his unfashionable, Adolf Hitler-style moustache. How could you believe a single word uttered by such a slovenly buffoon ?

'Yes,' continued Dover, gilding his non-existent lily with gusto, 'you and that clever bugger, Trevelyan, are in for a bit of an eye-opener. And a few others I could mention !'

A faint frown creased MacGregor's handsome brow. All bluff, of course. Dover wasn't capable of solving a problem to

183

which he'd already been given the answer. All this childish bragging was pathetic, really.

Wasn't it ?

MacGregor's frown deepened as he recalled that there had been occasions, albeit few and far between, when Dover had been right. It was an event comparable to monkeys with typewriters producing the Complete Works of William Shakespeare – unlikely but just possible. MacGregor's mind boggled as he tried once more to be scientific about it and work out the odds against this investigation ending in the usual shameful whimper. He stared hard at Dover who was still primping away in front of the fly-blown looking-glass. The flabby, pasty face was aglow with its usual expression of supreme self-confidence and self-satisfaction so that wasn't much help, but was there, perhaps, a faint gleam of intelligence in those mean, boot-button eyes ?

'You taken root or something ?' Dover had finished polishing the toes of his boots on the backs of his trousers and was now raring to go. 'His Nibs'll be bloody-minded enough without us keeping him waiting.'

MacGregor tore his mind away from Bath, Badminton and Bristol, kidnapped children and threats of mayhem to run a fastidious eye over Dover's unlovely figure. 'Your -er - flies are - er - undone, sir.'

Dover's stomach was rumbling with hunger. 'Trust you to go making a fuss about nothing !' He adjusted his clothing with clumsy fingers. 'There ! That suit you ?'

'Really, sir, it's not a question of suiting . . .'

Dover rumbled over MacGregor's bleated protest. 'These bloody zips aren't a patch on the old buttons. You knew where you were with buttons. They were slower, I grant you, but they were a hell of a lot safer. *And* things didn't keep getting caught in 'em,' he added obscurely.

But MacGregor wasn't listening. At long last the light was beginning to dawn. Bristol, Bath and Badminton ! Yes ! MacGregor slapped himself on the forehead in a gesture of mock reproach which was, nevertheless, more genuine than he cared to admit. Why in the name of heaven hadn't he seen the connection way back in Dover's office at the Yard when the three towns had been grouped together for the first time ? God knows, it was unlikely to solve the case with one wave of a magic wand but it should give them a more profitable lead than anything else had done so far. It was annoying that Dover should have been the one to stumble on the answer but MacGregor was modest enough to realise that he couldn't hog all the sagacity in the partnership all the time. In fact, being not only modest but amazingly generous as well, MacGregor was on the point of actually congratulating Dover on his perspicacity when that Grand Old Man of Detection cut short the conversation by opening the door of his bedroom and making his way with all possible speed downstairs towards the trough. The Assistant Commissioner (Crime) would no doubt be presiding over the luncheon table with all the charm of a death's head at the feast, but Dover reckoned that the man had not yet been born who could put him off his food.

In the event it was MacGregor who ruined everything. Instead of sitting there quietly as befitted his junior status in that August gathering, young Charles Edward had to go opening his trap and diving in with both flat feet.

The Assistant Commissioner (Crime) was still trying to slap the deafness out of his helicopter-battered ears and had barely had time to give vent to more than a couple of strings of oaths and three heavily sarcastic threats when he found himself being interrupted by a mere pup of a sergeant who ought to have known better. The Assistant Commissioner almost thought his poor old ears were deceiving him when, after the sketchiest of apologies, MacGregor launched into a short lesson on how to suck eggs.

'You *what*, sergeant ?'

MacGregor, although he was sitting some distance away at the bottom of the table, recoiled at the brusqueness with which he was addressed. The trouble was that the Assistant Commissioner was more than a little upset himself. He'd had a rotten morning, trying to explain to a bunch of hard-faced politicians why the combined efforts of every police force in the country had been unable to rescue one small child from the hands of a gang of kidnappers. The loss of that half a million pounds hadn't gone down too well, either, and the Home Secretary had made a very pointed remark about the British Public's penchant for scapegoats. And it was no good, he had added nastily, thinking that some junior police officer could be put forward as an acceptable burnt offering. No, the British Public (with some prompting, evidently, from the Home Secretary) was definitely going to demand a head with a gold-braided hat on it. For the first time in his life, the Assistant Commissioner felt a cold finger of fear running up and down his spine. As he felt every eye in that *ad hoc* committee turning to stare at him, he could find only one consolation : if he went, he bloody well wasn't going alone !

'You *what* ?'

MacGregor pulled himself together, if only to deprive his smirking neighbours of the joy of seeing him eaten alive. 'I was just wondering, actually, sir, if I could be excused for half an hour or so.'

'What for ?'

MacGregor tried in vain to catch Dover's eye. 'Well, I thought I might be of some assistance in getting things moving, sir. Time being, one imagines, of the - er - essence.'

The Assistant Commissioner couldn't have gone any blacker in the face than he was already. 'What things ?' he demanded tightly.

MacGregor dabbed his lips with a very clean white handkerchief. 'Hasn't Detective Chief Inspector Dover told you, sir ?' he asked feebly.

'As you may have observed, sergeant,' said the Assistant Commissioner through rigid lips, 'Detective Chief Inspector Dover has been too busy feeding his face to tell me anything.'

Dover, halfway down the table, looked up indignantly, a

hunk of bread in one hand and a spoon dripping soup in the other. 'Strewth, what was he supposed to do ? Let the bloody grub go cold ?

MacGregor floundered on from bad to worse. He shrugged his shoulders helplessly. 'I'm sorry, sir. I naturally assumed that everything would be well under way by now. I mean, Mr Dover's breakthrough did seem so remarkable that I almost thought we'd be restoring the child to its parents and locking up the Claret Tappers by now. I mean, I thought you'd want to get everything all tied up before the deadline for releasing those child murderers on Anglesey. I was sure . . .'

The Assistant Commissioner had borne more than any one man should be expected to bear. 'Sergeant,' he roared in a voice that set all the sauce bottles on the sideboard rattling, 'stop blethering !'

MacGregor's neighbours sniggered gleefully at his discomfiture and Dover, his bowl of soup as clean as a whistle, licked his spoon and looked round for what was coming next. There was a most delicious smell of steak and kidney pud . . .

'Dover !' screamed the Assistant Commissioner who was nearly in tears. 'I'm speaking to you, man ! What's all this about you having solved the case ?'

He might well ask. He wasn't, reflected Dover sadly, the only one who'd bloody well like to know. Solve the case ? That was the trouble with pompous young gits like MacGregor – they couldn't take a bloody joke.

The Assistant Commissioner's voice exploded down the length of the dining-room again. 'I'm still waiting, Dover !'

Dover's response this time was pure instinct. 'I think I'd better let young MacGregor here put you all in the picture,' he said with an air of sweet benevolence that made several of those present want to throw up. 'It'll be good practice for the lad in marshalling his ideas and expressing himself. My own part in the successful investigation of this case' – Dover cast his eyes down modestly – 'is really over now. I wish I could do more, but I'm afraid the old tripes are playing me up again. A legacy

187

from the war, you know,' Dover added for the benefit of the totally credulous in his audience. He nodded at MacGregor. 'Well, come on, laddie ! Let's be hearing from you !'

Having successfully dragged himself out of the mire by standing on his sergeant's head, Dover lost interest in that part of the proceedings. Grabbing his knife and fork in either hand, he smiled up ingratiatingly at the serving wench in the hope of getting an extra large helping of the steak and kidney.

MacGregor should, of course, have hit the ball straight back into Dover's teeth, but few of us can resist the opportunity to show off. MacGregor looked at the expectant faces round the table – all those senior police officers who could play such an effective role in furthering a young man's career . . .

MacGregor cleared his throat, smiled his most winning smile, straightened his tie and stood up. Fame and fortune, here we come ! 'Our main problem, gentlemen, has been our inability to get a line on the identity of the Claret Tappers. And, as you know only too well, apprehension without identification is a virtual impossibility.'

'Oh, get on with it, for Christ's sake !' The Assistant Commissioner took the words right out of Dover's mouth.

MacGregor swallowed his hasty retort like the sensible little policeman he was and tried again. 'To appreciate the situation fully, we have to go right back to the beginning . . .'

'Oh, no, we bloody don't !' This time the Assistant Commissioner's voice had quite a sharp edge to it.

MacGregor broke into a despairing gabble. 'Chief Inspector Dover was, unfortunately, unable to give us much help or information about the Claret Tappers. Not that any blame attaches to him for this,' he added hurriedly, taking thought for all the morrows Dover would have in which to wreak his revenge. 'The Claret Tappers took every precaution to ensure that the chief inspector neither saw nor heard anything which would betray them. So, gentlemen, we were obliged to look around for other avenues to explore. Now,' – MacGregor gulped in another great lungful of breath – 'you may recall that

188

the price demanded for Chief Inspector Dover's release was not only a considerable sum of money . . .'

'Which they didn't get !' broke in the Assistant Commissioner gleefully.

'. . . but the releasing of a couple of convicted criminals from prison as well.'

'Arthur Galsworthy and Elsie Whacker,' said Dover, just to let everybody know he was still there and kicking.

'Er – Archie Gallagher and Lesley Whittacker, actually, sir,' MacGregor corrected him as tactfully as possible. 'A bigamist and a shop-lifter, if you remember.'

The Assistant Commissioner reached for the mustard. 'I always said not enough attention was being paid to those two.'

'We did interview both prisoners, sir,' said MacGregor, 'and questioned them very closely. The trouble was that we didn't appreciate the significance of what they told us. We came away from the interviews feeling that we had learned precisely . . . nothing.'

'Has anybody ever told you that you ought to be on the stage, sergeant ?' asked Superintendent Trevelyan. 'Even country bumpkins like us can see that your talents are wasted in the police.'

This remark brought a few appreciative sniggers from the superintendent's cronies, but MacGregor pressed on as though there had been no interruption. 'In actual fact, however, the chief inspector and I had been handed our first clue on – if I may coin a phrase – a plate.'

Dover nodded enthusiastically and went on scraping out the vegetable dishes.

'Both Gallagher and Whittacker revealed the vital facts in almost casual asides . . .'

'Can't say I remember Elsie Whacker revealing any vital facts !' observed Dover trying to curry cheap popularity by pretending to be something of a dog.

MacGregor let his frustration show at last. 'If I could continue without these continual interruptions,' he said icily.

'Now, Archie Gallagher let the fact drop that he had been arrested for bigamy at Badminton and Miss Whittacker told us that she had stood her trial at Bristol. Both prisoners were tried at much the same time, some twelve months earlier.'

Dover paused with a heavily loaded fork half-way to his mouth. Well, he'd be damned ! So that was what MacGregor had been yacking on about ! Dover had no intention, of course, of letting his sergeant enjoy his moment of glory and proceeded to steal the pitiful thunder without a qualm. 'In other words, they were both brought to trial and sentenced at the same Crown Court !'

'Yes,' agreed MacGregor unhappily as all eyes swung round to stare at Dover. 'Bristol Crown Court is the link we were looking for.'

'The link between Whittacker and Gallagher,' corrected the Assistant Commissioner sharply. He was looking far from starry-eyed. 'I fail to see how you tie this up with the Claret Tappers.'

'It's my guess, sir,' – MacGregor felt Dover's irate glance on him and corrected himself submissively – 'it's *our* guess, sir, that the Claret Tappers must have been present at that session of the court. How else would they have known about Whittacker and Gallagher ?'

The landlord's wife was clearing away the empty plates while the waitress brought the pudding course in. Superintendent Trevelyan accepted his dish of Spotted Dick but made no attempt to eat it. 'I don't get it !' he complained. 'Surely the Claret Tappers had some proper reason for wanting those two cons sprung. Why make it a condition of Dover's release otherwise ?'

MacGregor leaned excitedly across the table, only too happy to sort things out for the superintendent. 'Ah, that's what we thought at first, sir, but it's clear now that all this business about freeing prisoners from jail or Broadmoor patients is just another red herring. The Claret Tappers were trying to confuse the picture, you see, and I must say' – MacGregor very considerately didn't look at Dover – 'they succeeded.'

The Assistant Commissioner refused the Spotted Dick and accepted ice-cream in lieu. He waved his spoon in an arc which more or less included Dover. 'Not bad,' he acknowledged grudgingly.

'Not bad ?' repeated Dover irately. The police officer sitting next to him was on a diet so there was a plate of Spotted Dick going spare and the chief inspector didn't want to miss it. ''Strewth, it's bloody marvellous !'

'And that's not all, sir,' said MacGregor.

'Too right it isn't !' agreed Dover, finding to his great delight that his other neighbour was worrying about his waistline, too. Three puds for the price of one ! Smashing ! Dover's plate was soon running over. 'Tell 'em the rest, laddie !' he advised as he sank his spoon into that gorgeous, melting, soggy mess. 'And don't be so bloody long-winded about it !'

MacGregor had been sitting on the files which he had rescued from Dover's clutches and he now, with some contortions, produced them. 'The girl . . .' – he flipped anxiously through the pages – 'the one who took a job in the Yard canteen as a waitress and who, we believe, tipped off the kidnappers when Chief Inspector Dover was leaving and . . . Ah, Miss Mary Jones ! An obvious alias.'

Several of the listening policemen had lit up cigarettes and Dover risked choking himself as he gobbled up his afters, hoping to have consumed all before the cigarette packets were put away.

'Now, Miss Mary Jones,' MacGregor went on, unaware that he had eaten and drunk practically nothing at lunch, 'was a very elusive young lady.' He gave a bit of a laugh but, if this was an attempt to liven up the proceedings, it failed. The smoking, tooth-picking coppers were growing somnolent and the yawns were coming thicker and faster than the grunts of professional appreciation. 'In fact,' admitted MacGregor ruefully, 'virtually all we were able to find out about her was that she owned a coat which had been bought in Bath.'

The Assistant Commissioner forced his eyes open and rubbed the back of his neck vigorously. 'Fascinating !' he said and glared down the table at Dover who, with the Spotted Dick still damp on his lapels, was busy cadging a fag off his next-door neighbour. 'Another connection with the - er - West Country, of course.'

'That's right, sir! We checked with the shopkeeper who sold the coat but she was unable to remember anything helpful. Still, it's the West Country connection that counts - as you so cleverly saw, sir. It's really the clincher in my opinion. It proves that that's the part of the world we ought to be looking for the Claret Tappers in. And,' concluded MacGregor triumphantly, 'Salisbury and Fish Down aren't a thousand miles from Bath, are they ?'

'About forty, actually,' said Superintendent Trevelyan, who was not alone in having difficulty keeping his eyes open.

'Well,' asked the Assistant Commissioner, 'what are you waiting for ?'

'Sir ?'

The Assistant Commissioner dropped the third spoonful of sugar into his coffee. 'If the solution to the kidnapping lies in Bristol or wherever, what the hell are you doing sitting here ? This business is supposed to be getting the very top priority, sergeant. It's the Prime Minister's grandson who's been snatched, not some crummy nobody we've never heard of.' The Assistant Commissioner tasted his coffee and grimaced. It was cold and bitter. 'Well, get moving, sergeant !' he roared.

MacGregor all but ruptured himself scrambling to his feet. 'I'm on my way, sir !'

The Assistant Commissioner (Crime) bawled a final instruction: 'And take Dover with you !'

Sixteen

It was three days before MacGregor caught up with Dover – not that he'd been trying all that hard. The touching reunion took place in their poky office at Scotland Yard. MacGregor just opened the door and . . .

'Where the bloody hell do you think you've been ?'

MacGregor realised that he'd come home at last. He closed the door behind him. 'I'm terribly sorry, sir,' he began.

'*Sorry?*' Dover was going to need a great deal more in the way of reparations than that. 'You miserable little rat !'

'It was hardly my fault, sir,' protested MacGregor. 'I managed to make the superintendent wait all of ten minutes, but after that I just couldn't hold him.'

'Blackleg !' roared Dover. 'You knew where I was !'

This was true and MacGregor didn't attempt to deny it. The fact was that in the middle of the mass stampede to fulfil the Assistant Commissioner's orders and get to Bristol, Dover had thrown a tiny spanner in the works by announcing that he would have to pay a short visit before undertaking the journey. Ignoring the protests that this statement aroused, he had ambled off to the downstairs gents' – and as far as anybody knew had remained there.

'When I came out,' Dover grumbled on as he watched MacGregor squeeze into the chair behind his desk, 'you'd all gone.'

'I'm sorry, sir. I assumed that you'd follow us.'

'I did !' snarled Dover. 'All over the bloody country. Every time I arrived anywhere, you bloody lot had moved on somewhere else.'

MacGregor permitted himself the faintest shrug of his shoulders. 'Once we got the first clue, sir, we had to get a move on. The child's life could have been in deadly danger.'

'Never mind that it was my bloody case,' said Dover with an aggrieved sniff. 'Never mind that I was the one who bloody solved it. Ho, no, when it comes to collecting the glory, I can be elbowed aside like an old glove and have the cup of triumph dashed from my lips. And all because of an acute attack of diarrhoea.'

'Oh, *sir*!' moaned MacGregor who was finding it hard coming back to this sort of thing after his three days of freedom. He reached for his universal remedy. 'Would you like a cigarette, sir ?'

Dover's eager hand was already out. 'Thought you were never going to ask !' he rumbled. 'Well, go on, laddie ! Tell us what happened !'

'Happened, sir ?' Even MacGregor couldn't believe that Dover didn't know the whole story already. 'Didn't you read about it in the newspapers ?'

'What bloody chance have I had to read newspapers ?' demanded Dover reasonably enough. 'The way I've been dashing around . . .'Strewth, I haven't had my boots off for forty-eight hours and . . .'

MacGregor decided not to waste any more time. 'Well, sir, with the arrest of the last Claret Tapper this morning, I think we can say that it's all over. Everything's pretty well tied up.'

'Don't spare me any of the boring details !' advised Dover unpleasantly. 'I've got to sit here till five o'clock whatever happens.'

194

'Superintendent Trevelyan and I went to Bristol, sir.'

'Taking every bloody police car with you,' interrupted Dover, 'as I know to my cost. Would you believe it took those peasants more than two bloody hours to rustle up some transport for me? If I hadn't pulled my rank on 'em I'd be sitting in that lousy pub yet.'

'Couldn't you have caught a train, sir? I believe there's quite a good service from . . .'

Dover stared at his sergeant as though the young ponce had suddenly sprouted two heads. 'Trains cost money, you moron! What am I supposed to be doing? Subsidising the bloody tax-payers now?'

'Sorry, sir. I hadn't thought of that.' MacGregor swung his chair round and stared out of the window. Perhaps if he didn't have to look at the old fool . . . 'Well, when we reached Bristol, sir, we went straight to the Crown Court where the fellow in charge of the records had all the paperwork ready and waiting for us. Superintendent Trevelyan had seen to that.' MacGregor permitted himself a faint grin at the memory. 'The superintendent has a very forceful technique on the car radio. He certainly knows how to get things moving. He even got us a motor-cycle escort to take us through the town and . . .' A little late in the day MacGregor realised that all this enthusiasm for the superintendent must sound to some large and flapping ears like the blackest treachery. He hurried to make amends. 'We soon found that your deductions were absolutely correct, sir. Gallagher and Whittacker had, indeed, stood trial during the same week and had actually been put up for sentencing on the same day. Just over a year ago. Well, that seemed the obvious place to start and we immediately began to check on all the other people who were around the Crown Court at about that time. As a temporary measure, we decided to ignore people like solicitors and barristers and newspaper reporters and such like, and concentrated on other accused persons and . . .'

'. . . to cut a long story short,' said Dover, dropping his hint like a ton of bricks.

'We found this group of yobboes, sir,' said MacGregor with a sigh. 'They stood out like a handful of sore thumbs. It was all too easy, really. One of them – Freddie Collins – was accused of stealing a car and all the rest of the jokers had rallied round to give him an alibi. I've read the reports of the trial since, sir, and Collins was as guilty as hell, if you ask me.'

'But he got off ?'

'The jury found him "not guilty", sir,' agreed MacGregor. 'In view of his subsequent activities and those of his companions, I think we can chalk that one up as a gross miscarriage of justice.'

Dover grunted. 'Nothing new about that, laddie ! Miscarriages of justice ? 'Strewth, if I was to tell you how many times I've suffered from that sort of thing, you wouldn't bloody well believe me !'

'No, sir,' said MacGregor. 'I don't suppose I would.'

Dover had a quick look to see if the cocky little squirt was trying to take the mickey and decided, reluctantly, that perhaps he wasn't. 'I do wish you'd get on with it !' he complained.

'Well, that's really all there is to it, sir. Superintendent Trevelyan got weaving on the blower and the local police did a simultaneous swoop and brought in all the people connected with this Freddie Collins case. Once they were questioned in depth, Freddie Collins and his two accomplices stood out so clearly that nobody could have missed them. They'd been so sure of pulling it off, you see, that they hadn't bothered to concoct a worthwhile story. It's funny, really, because their planning had been meticulous in almost every other respect.'

Dover was looking puzzled. 'But they'd got the ransom money,' he objected. 'Half a million nicker ! By the time you caught up with 'em, they'd had it for hours. Why hadn't they just dropped everything and scarpered ? 'Strewth, if I ever got that much lolly in my hands' – his eyes misted over at the thought – 'you wouldn't see me for bloody dust !'

'Perhaps not, sir,' said MacGregor, his boredom momentarily making him a little careless, 'but the Claret Tappers

196

were cleverer than that. They didn't want to spend the rest of their days in some stinking South American town, waiting for the law to catch up with them. It's no fun being a fugitive. Their plan was simply to sit tight until all the fuss had died down. Then they were going to move quietly to another part of the country where nobody knew them and only then start spending the money. No, I reckon the Claret Tappers have been pretty clever about most of the things they've done.'

'Clever?' scoffed Dover. 'What do you mean – clever? I don't call it clever to go around and get yourself bloody caught!' He puffed his chest out. 'They weren't as clever as *me*, laddie!'

'I merely meant that they always tried to do the unusual or the unexpected, sir. After all, who would ever have thought of kidnapping a high-ranking detective from Scotland Yard in the first place? You've got to admit that was original. Or of letting him go unharmed when they realised that they weren't going to collect any ransom money for him?'

'Bah, typical commie student stuff!'

MacGregor shook his head. 'And that's another thing, sir. The Claret Tappers aren't left-wing, neo-Maoist students at all. Collins himself works in a shoe shop and Hamilton is a Gas Board employee. The third chap worked in a factory until he was made redundant and the girl – our "Mary Jones" – is a freelance shorthand-typist. They just wanted everybody to get the impression that they were a bunch of way-out students so as to lay yet another false trail. That's why they made these rather absurd demands for the release of convicted prisoners and criminal lunatics. And why they sent their messages through the Archbishop of Canterbury and silly things like that.' MacGregor noticed that Dover's eyelids were beginning to droop and raised his voice out of sheer spite. 'And that's why, sir, they timed their kidnappings to coincide with the university vacations. They kidnapped you at Christmas and the Prime Minister's grandson at Easter, if you remember. All in all they spared no effort to send us all haring off in quite the wrong direction.'

'Didn't fool me for a bloody minute,' claimed Dover sleepily. 'I didn't go haring off after anybody.'

There was no disputing the truth of that statement and MacGregor couldn't help reflecting that really conscientious and imaginative criminals were wasted on Dover. He abandoned such treasonable thoughts quickly, however, when he realised he was being addressed. 'Oh – er – I beg your pardon, sir ?'

'I asked you,' said Dover crossly, 'where you found the kid. You growing cloth ears or something ?'

'The Prime Minister's grandchild, sir ? Oh, the Claret Tappers had coped with that rather neatly, too, I thought. You remember our "Mary Jones", sir ? The girl in the canteen ? Well, her real name is Jean Hamilton and she's the sister of one of the men in the gang, but I'll call her "Mary Jones" to make things easier for you.'

'Oh, ta very much !'

MacGregor took a deep breath and reminded himself that not thumping somebody in the teeth was a positive Christian virtue. 'It was Mary Jones's job to look after the baby, sir. Did I tell you she was not only Hamilton's sister but also the girl friend of Freddie Collins.'

'The baby was ?' asked Dover, waking up as he got the chance to display his wit. 'Well, you do surprise me ! I thought the kid was a boy !'

MacGregor kept his face icily expressionless. One day, though . . . 'Mary Jones took the Prime Minister's kidnapped grandchild to Weston-super-Mare, sir. She has an aunt there who runs a seaside boarding house. Mary Jones went to stay with her. It's off-season, you see, so there was plenty of room.'

'The aunt must be a nutter,' objected Dover, hunting through all his desk drawers on the off-chance that there was something edible lurking there. 'The papers were full of that brat being nicked.' He slammed the last fruitless drawer shut. 'Didn't it occur to the old cow to put two and bloody two

198

together when her niece turned up with a baby ?'

MacGregor knew the answer to that question and, in his eagerness to share this knowledge with Dover, he leaned forward eagerly across his desk. Dover, a great humourist, chose to react as though an assault was about to be made upon his virtue and MacGregor, helplessly watching all those moppings and mowings of mock alarm, chalked up yet another grievance against the disgusting old pig. Gritting his teeth, he resumed his seat with as much dignity as he could. 'The aunt thought the baby was Mary Jones's child, sir. Apparently Miss Jones had produced an illegitimate infant – a girl, as it happens – some six months ago. The aunt knew about this but what she didn't know was that the baby had been adopted almost immediately after it had been born. There'd been some sort of family disagreement or other and the aunt in Weston-super-Mare wasn't on speaking terms with the rest of the family.'

'A likely story !' guffawed Dover. 'Blimey, if you believe that, you'll believe anything ! You want to get old Auntie in and thump the living daylights out of her. She'd tell you a different tale then.'

'I'm afraid we can't touch her, sir. She says she didn't know and Mary Jones says she didn't know. Unless we can find some proof that she did know . . .' MacGregor shrugged his shoulders.

'Was the Prime Minister's brat in good nick ?' asked Dover without much interest.

'Oh, yes, sir. He'd been well looked after. Whatever else the Claret Tappers are, they're not monsters.'

'They killed that au pair girl,' Dover pointed out sourly.

'They claim that was a most unfortunate accident, sir.'

'And what about the brutal and sadistic way they treated me ?' demanded Dover, alighting on a subject more up his street. 'I still haven't recovered from the inhuman treatment I received at their hands. To say nothing of having to climb up that bloody mountain with the bloody ransom money.' Dover interrupted his threnody for lost health to make a heart-

199

rending appeal. 'You got a bar of chocolate on you, laddie ? Or anything to eat ? Well, don't just sit there shaking your bloody head ! Have a look through your pockets to make sure.'

MacGregor obediently went through the motions though he was perfectly sure that the pockets of his expensively tailored suit contained neither scotch eggs, packets of sandwiches nor even the odd cream cake. Very tentatively he made the obvious suggestion. 'The canteen, sir ?'

Dover's scowl deepened. 'They're on bloody strike ! Don't you know anything ?' He slumped back in his chair. 'Oh, well, you might as well get on with your story. Maybe it'll take my mind off things.'

'Actually, sir, I don't think there's much more to tell. We found the ransom money, still intact in the mail-bags, in a garden shed at Collins's house. The Claret Tappers weren't going to make any attempt to spend it until what they called the heat was well and truly off. They said they were prepared to wait eighteen months or two years, even. They'd got it all planned out.'

'You sound as though you've got a soft spot for these young thugs !'

MacGregor took time off to give this accusation some serious consideration. Nobody who'd thought of kidnapping Dover could be all bad, of course, but on the other hand they had let the old devil go again. It was hard to forgive thoughtless behaviour like that. MacGregor shook his head. 'The Claret Tappers are just a bunch of cheap crooks like all the rest of 'em, sir. Greedy and lazy.'

The most idle and avaricious policeman in the United Kingdom (and, possibly, the world) nodded his head in righteous agreement. 'Do anything for money except bloody work,' he said.

'Precisely, sir.' MacGregor took a surreptitious glance at his watch. Good heavens, was that all it was ? He could have sworn he'd been sitting there for hours and hours, not just a twenty-five lousy minutes.

200

Dover's mind, meanwhile, had latched onto happier fantasies. 'Was it you that found the ransom money?' he asked enviously.

'Superintendent Trevelyan and I, sir. Once the Claret Tappers realised that we were on to them and that the game was up, they became quite cooperative. I think the death of that au pair girl upset them quite a lot.'

'You and Trevelyan, eh?' Disappointed, Dover helped himself to another of MacGregor's cigarettes. 'Pity.'

'Sir?'

'Skip it! What about that horse thing?'

'Horse thing, sir?'

'Jesus!' exploded Dover. 'Sometimes you strike me as being thicker than a couple of bloody planks. The horse thing I had to climb that bloody mountain to tie the money bags on the lousy back of! What else, for God's sake?'

'Oh, the Shetland pony, sir?' MacGregor's face brightened as comprehension dawned. 'Oh, it's fine as far as I am aware, sir. None the worse for its experiences, you know.'

'Very humorous!' snarled Dover, who could always be relied on to see a joke and take umbrage at it. 'How did the Claret Tappers come to use the nasty little brute?'

'Oh, one of the lads – Joe Buller, the redundant factory worker – had spent a sort of working holiday at harvest time last year on the next-door farm, sir. He's a bit more *au fait* with the country than the others are and he realised that the pony, once it was untied, would lose no time in taking the shortest way home for its breakfast. The Claret Tappers knew we wouldn't hand over all that cash without at least trying to follow them, so they took a few precautions. They assumed – quite rightly, as it turned out – that we would place all our hopes on an unobtrusive surveillance of the roads. Well, in that particular area, there was very little else we could do. The Claret Tappers simply came up with a collection method which didn't use the roads at all – or not roads that were passable for cars. Actually, the one thing which would have foxed

201

them would have been a helicopter hovering overhead, but, if they'd spotted any kind of aircraft in the vicinity, they would have called the whole operation off.'

'And killed the kid ?'

'Well, they say not, sir, but your guess is as good as mine.'

'Better !' sniggered Dover.

'And they do point out, sir, that they didn't kill you when the ransom money wasn't forthcoming.'

'I'm well aware they didn't kill me, laddie !' snapped Dover. A feeling of tiredness seemed to be creeping over him and making him more fractious than usual. 'What about . . . ?' The end of the question sank without trace in an unhibited yawn.

'What about what, sir ?'

Dover was blowed if he could remember, so he gave expression to something else that had been on his mind for some time. 'I suppose they'll be dishing a few medals out for this business, eh ?'

'Medals, sir ?' MacGregor picked an invisible piece of lint off the sleeve of his jacket. 'What on earth for ?'

'For deeds of bravery and endurance beyond the call of bloody duty !' snapped Dover. 'Some of us have sacrificed our health and strength on this particular battlefield.'

MacGregor got a piece of paper out of his drawer and unscrewed the cap of his fountain pen. His next claim for expenses was going to need some working out. 'Well, there might be the odd commendation, sir, I suppose. Seeing that there were VIPs involved.'

'Well, even that'd be better than a slap in the belly with a wet fish,' said Dover, wondering if MacGregor had been taking private lessons in obtuseness.

MacGregor got his notebook out. 'Now you come to mention it, sir, I believe I did hear some talk about Superintendent Trevelyan being in line for something.'

'Would you bloody believe it ?' demanded Dover, his jowls quivering with rage and disappointment.

'It wasn't a commendation, though, sir.'

202

Dover clutched his head. 'Not a cash reward ?'

'A personal letter from the Prime Minister, I think, sir.'

'And that's all ?'

'To the best of my knowledge, sir.'

Dover folded his arms across his chest and issued his final pronouncement, not only on the kidnappings but upon life as he saw it in general. 'There's no bloody justice !' he said.